hurt hawks

hurt hawks
BY MIKE MINER

"Wars never really end; the fight just follows you home. In **HURT HAWKS**, Mike Miner brings the battlefield to Dorchester, Massachusetts, steeping his tale of revenge and honor in deep New England roots. It's like if Harry Brown (and a few of his closest pals) lived in a Dennis Lehane novel. With lean, exacting prose and imagery that cuts to the bone, Miner shows what life is like when the bombs fade and the smoke drifts away. Because a new enemy is always ready to take the place of the old, and men born to fight do what they do best: they survive. Or they die trying."
> —**Joe Clifford**, author of *Junkie Love* and *Lamentation*

"Miner's **HURT HAWKS** is like well-aged bourbon. It's smooth, smoky but with a kick! There are hints of Frederick Forsyth's Dogs of War and a very pleasing Elmore Leonard after taste. It's an action-packed noir beauty. Kick off your shoes and drink it straight."
> —**Joe Gannon**, author of *Night of the Jaguar*

Mike Miner's prose style is as spare as the final round in your last magazine and as singular in purpose. **HURT HAWKS** is propelled most of all by great characterization. Add to that a very timely setting, and a story that echoes both the tragic and heroic elements of Yojimbo and Seven Samurai, and this book is a shot that hits the mark.
> —**Bracken MacLeod**, author of *Mountain Home*

ALSO BY
Mike Miner

The Immortal Game

The Hurt Business

Prodigal Sons

True Dark

hurt hawks

MIKE MINER

Published by **Shotgun Honey Books**

215 Loma Road
Charleston, WV 25314
www.ShotgunHoney.com

Cover Design by Bad Fido.

ISBN-10: 1-956957-35-9
ISBN-13: 978-1-956957-35-8

11 10 9 8 7 6 5 4 3   24 23 22 21 20 19 18

*This book is dedicated to the villains.
Where would our heroes be without them?*

hurt hawks

Hurt Hawks

Robinson Jeffers

I.

The broken pillar of the wing jags from the clotted shoulder,
The wing trails like a banner in defeat,
No more to use the sky forever but live with famine
And pain a few days: cat nor coyote
Will shorten the week of waiting for death, there is game without talons.
He stands under the oak-bush and waits
The lame feet of salvation; at night he remembers freedom
And flies in a dream, the dawns ruin it.
He is strong and pain is worse to the strong, incapacity is worse.
The curs of the day come and torment him
At distance, no one but death the redeemer will humble that head,
The intrepid readiness, the terrible eyes.
The wild God of the world is sometimes merciful to those
That ask mercy, not often to the arrogant.
You do not know him, you communal people, or you have forgotten him;
Intemperate and savage, the hawk remembers him;
Beautiful and wild, the hawks, and men that are dying, remember him.

ONE

_

IF HE COMES, WHEN HE COMES, Chris Rogers will kill him.

The man will bring others. Chris will kill them too. The man is coming to rob Chris, to kill him, to take his wife. The others the man will bring because he is a coward. They will be well paid. Their deaths will pass unmourned.

Chris sits in his wheelchair, in his small convenience store in Dorchester, Massachusetts. His father's store and before that, his grandfather's store. A rifle lays across his ruined lap. In a shoulder strap, his Glock is holstered, loaded and ready.

A long time since he fired a weapon. Not since the desert.

Behind the store, in the attached house, his wife and son sleep. They want nothing to do with Chris. He can't blame them. The soldier who went off to Afghanistan did not return. He is a jigsaw puzzle missing all the important pieces. His legs didn't make it back. He isn't sure all of his mind did either.

His dog, Sam, is at his side. Part of his therapy, a helper animal. Sam did not know Chris before the war. The dog accepts his master as is, unconditionally. The feeling is mutual.

A drug induced fog haunts his brain. Pain killers, psychotropics, for this evening's event he has doubled up. Real life and dream life merge and overlap. He is only half awake.

In real life, Chris was a hero. His hands never shook, his mind never wavered. He saw the Afghan soldier aim his rifle at an American officer.

A perfect shot took the Afghan out.

In his dreams, Chris is a coward. He hides and watches as the Afghan takes the American out. In his dreams, Chris returns home with no injuries, no pieces missing. He can walk, he can run. He can lift his son up and toss him high, then catch him in an embrace. No pills. No dogs instead of friends. He can make love to his wife.

In his dreams.

Real life always comes knocking, every morning, to chop off his legs.

The rifle is no longer in his lap.

The man he planned on killing holds it. He looks

from the gun to Chris. He winks. Looks back at the rifle. Whistles.

"Hey, Nate."

"Hey, Chris. This is a serious piece of equipment."

Nate's left eye squints, doesn't look in the same direction as the right one. He is squat, not more than five feet seven inches, with the proportions of a dwarf; huge head, barrel torso, long arms and short legs. A shape that hasn't changed much in the twenty or so years they have known each other.

The store is dim. Chris's vision is blurry. Two or three men lurk behind him. He senses their menace, a nasty scent in the air, like something burning. The weight of the pistol is still there, under his arm.

Nate paints his face with regret, like a reluctant messenger. "You know, Chris." He can't quite lose his smile though. "Pay us our fee and you won't need a piece of equipment like this. We'll protect you."

From ourselves, Chris reads between the lines.

"But you gotta be a tough guy. A hard case."

Chris stares at the ground. Looks for his dog.

"This ain't school anymore, pal. You're not homecoming king anymore, not dancing with the prom queen." Nate giggles. "Shit, I guess you're not dancing with anyone anymore."

The others join the laughter.

The dog Sam sidles up next to Nate. Chris grins. Nate looks at the dog, moves his hand to pet it. Sam sinks his teeth into Nate's offered hand. A shelter animal, the one rule is to move your hand toward Sam from below. Anything from above he will take as a threat.

"Son of a bitch." Nate draws a hand cannon out of a holster and shoots the mutt.

The ruckus gives Chris a chance to draw his piece. He starts shooting, his chest a riot of adrenaline and drugs, his heart pumps fast, his extremities tingle, even his phantom legs.

The gun is empty but Chris keeps firing. In his head, he's back in Kandahar. Bullets whiz past his head, the night a Van Gogh painting of explosions, a symphony of violence.

Then Nate stands in front of him. Not the adult version but the squinty-eyed child Chris used to tease on the playground, the kid with all that hate in his eyes and the chip on his shoulder. The boy with a crush on his future wife. He looks at Chris with something like pity before he shoots him in the heart.

TWO

—

MR. SILVER HAS TRADED one desert for another. He's gotten used to the scenery. The big sky, a land of horizons, comforts him now. Cities make him claustrophobic, but Vegas has the view he craves. This landscape allows him to keep his bitterness close. After his military career blew up, along with his foot, bitterness is all he has left.

He walks with a cane now, like another famous pirate. He's taken his name. Silver. L.J. Silver. At your service. Maybe he was always a pirate. Now he owns the title. Officially he runs security for various fat cats. Military contractors, arms dealers, a few cartel jefes. Does their dirty deeds, washes their dirty laundry, guards them, hires their help, and supplies them with weapons. A middle man. A bag man. A mercenary. A pirate.

Why not?

He is well compensated. Why should he care how dirty the money is?

If he didn't do it, wouldn't someone else? That's what he tells his conscience after a few drinks.

Being a hero just got your limbs blown off. Ask Chris Rogers.

Silver is in an extravagant suite in the Bellagio Hotel. Bosses from Colombia, Mexico and the Cosa Nostra sit in leather chairs. Like the start of a bad joke, Silver thinks; a Colombian, a Mexican and an Italian walk into a room. The producer, the supplier, the buyer. They meet once a year. Silver sets up the meet. The room has been swept three times for bugs. The last time by him personally. He has two other rooms reserved in two other casinos, same catering spread, same everything. Smoke screens.

The three bosses complain about their wives, they brag about their kids. Just like regular folks do, Silver supposes, though he wouldn't know. No wife or kids for him. These are not regular guys. These men have murdered dozens, ordered the deaths of hundreds, they run guns, drugs and women across the border. Their souls are deep in the devil's pocket. Just like Silver's.

The three men puff on cigars. Cubans, a gift from the Colombian, Alejandro.

Silver stands apart, sips from a glass of Remy Martin. He enjoys having a job that allows him to have a stiff morning drink without raising any eyebrows. He is labor not management in this meeting though he is trusted enough to hear what they discuss. A logistics man, they often ask his opinion.

"Sit, Johnny," the Cosa Nostra man, Giovanni Junior, GJ, tells him. A heavy man, in a perfectly tailored blue Canali suit, white shirt, white tie with a matching pocket triangle, GJ maintains a fatherly aspect. He seems sentimental but Silver has seen his temper, knows how quick it can rise.

Silver taps his cane, nods and sits.

"The new border patrol budget is *chingado*, it's fucked," says José from the Mexican mafia. He has not stopped eating since he entered the room. One look tells Silver this is a man of uncontrolled appetites, a man who takes what he can grab. The scars on his face show he is willing to pay the price for what he takes. He speaks with his mouth full. "The tighter security changes the routes of my burros. The ones that don't get caught get lost in the Sonoran Desert."

"That's a real waste of my product," the Colombian, Alejandro, says. His voice is deep, his eyes are sleepy.

Silver has not dealt with Alejandro before. He makes Silver nervous. Like a coiled snake, the Colombian is ready to strike. Something off about him. A few years too young. A few pounds too light. He doesn't move like a boss, he moves like an assassin.

"A terrible waste," José says.

GJ clears his throat. "So less drugs are costing more money."

"So it seems." José eyes the desserts.

The Mexican doesn't realize what Silver just realized. José won't be walking out of this meeting.

GJ says, "I suppose that's the price of doing business."

José offers an apologetic smile.

"Gentlemen." Alejandro stands, slow and lazy, stretches his legs. "How about a drink?"

Silver makes to stand.

Alejandro, too quick, motions for him to stay seated.

"Relax, Johnny."

Silver puts his hands up in surrender.

Alejandro gives him a look that says, *Are you cool with this?*

Silver shrugs, *Of course.*

Alejandro nods. "What can I get you, *amigos*?"

"Sambuca for me," GJ says.

"*Patrón, si puedes, amigo.*"

"*Claro que sí.*"

The bar, fully stocked, is right behind José. Silver remembers GJ and Alejandro arriving early. He should have known then. He's slipping.

The Italian looks melancholy, resigned. Alejandro's eyes, no longer sleepy, are wide and happy. He whistles as he brings the other two their drinks.

"To another successful year." Alejandro raises his glass.

"*Salúd*," José says. He tilts his crystal glass back.

One bullet in the chest. One in the face. Two soft coughs from the silenced pistol. José drops onto the thick carpet. Even the glass falling barely makes a sound. A nice, quiet death. The gun is put away as fast as it was drawn.

Alejandro and GJ toast each other and drink.

GJ turns to face Silver. "You don't look surprised."

"When did you know?" Alejandro looks curious. Did he tip his hand too soon?

"Less drugs are costing more money." Silver knows the bottom line in this business, the only line.

Alejandro purses his lips. "You were a soldier, yes?"

"Yes."

"You have been tested in battle. It shows."

Silver raises his glass and sips it. "I will take care of the mess." He's seen worse. Much worse. Again he thinks of Chris Rogers. Why? Now maimed in a wheelchair, nursing visible and invisible scars. Silver remembers the screams, the young soldier's mangled legs. Remembers thinking, *What have I done?* Bullets can do worse than kill sometimes.

Silver's missing foot itches today, like a guilty conscience. He would have to go to Afghanistan to scratch it. To Kandahar. So Silver knows it is an itch that will never be scratched.

The gangster and the killer finish their drinks.

"Tell me," GJ talks to Silver. "How would you handle the new border regulations?"

Silver smiles. "Last I checked, the border patrol is not made up entirely of saints. Find the right men, open a new path. Pay more to ensure more product gets through."

"A practical man," Alejandro says. "The good things I heard about you are true, Señor Silver." He grins. "Tell me, I am always curious. How did you wind up doing this? Your father was a soldier maybe?"

"Yes."

"And now?"

"He owns a small store in New England."

"But this was not for you, right? A *caballero*."

A cowboy. "I reckon."

Alejandro finishes his drink. "Some days, I wager that little store looks pretty good."

"Some days."

"Today?"

"Today, I'll make more money than he does in a year."

"Yes, the money. Covers all manner of sins, sí?"

"Sí."

"*Hasta luego, amigo*."

As Silver shakes hands with these despicable people, he wonders what has happened. When did he become such a bad person? Is he bad or just indifferent? Numb, he decides.

He remembers himself as a boy, so anxious to escape his small New England home town. His father, a Yankee merchant, owner of the general store in town, a Vietnam vet. How could he be happy following the same routine day after day? His mother tended the yard, made the meals, sighed, her eyes tired, bored, sad. He did not want their lives, did not understand them. Did not want to settle for a life. Just get by.

School did nothing for him. Classrooms and chalk dust made him sleepy. So he enlisted. Army, like his dad.

Marching. Running. Obstacle courses. Drills. Guns. Silver loved it. His body responded like a perfectly calibrated machine. Who knew? His scores were off the charts. Set the camp record on the obstacle course. His range scores were unreal, his bullets, like bullseye magnets, never missed.

He was sent to be made a Ranger at Fort Benning, Georgia, with three thousand other guys, give or take. A collection of gung-ho grunts too young to know they could be killed. Special Forces. They all thought they were invincible, bullet proof. Some of them were. Like Silver.

More running - harder, faster, more weapons training – bigger, more dangerous, vehicle training. Silver jumped out of dozens of perfectly good airplanes. Learned a hundred ways to kill another human being.

He itched for combat.

His battalion was shipped to the Mojave Desert in California. They learned how to survive in the desert, how to read and draw maps. In his spare time, Silver learned Farsi, a tongue twisting mess of a language.

Silver was already in Kuwait City when war was declared.

War.

As wars go, nothing special. The Iraqis didn't put up much of a fight. Like a school yard bully when the teacher catches them. They rolled over.

Combat.

It cannot be fabricated. Simulations come only so close. Until the bullets fly, until the tanks roll, you don't know if you have what it takes. Silver had it. In spades. Cool and calm under fire. A natural leader, he had a nose for his opponent's weak spots. He trusted his instincts and before long, his fellow soldiers did too.

He remembers pitying men who never found their calling in life. He smiles now at his young self. Should have saved all that pity. For himself.

Silver inspects José's lifeless corpse. Not too messy. He has the tools he needs. A thick plastic tarp. Bleach and other cleaning supplies. A rolling luggage rack. He knows a discreet way to get the body to a dumpster.

José's head lolls, his face looks at Silver with a twisted leer. Silver suspects there would be no dental records to match, but he's a thorough man. He's paid to be. He finds his pliers and begins to yank the man's teeth out of his head.

His phone vibrates. A number he doesn't recognize. A 617 prefix. Massachusetts. This is his personal phone. A number he's kept for years, unlike the work phones he disposes of after each job. Less than ten people know this number. He hesitates. Presses *talk*. "Hello?"

A woman's voice. "Is this Captain Donovan?"

It used to be, Silver thinks. Captain Patrick Donovan.

"Are you there?" A desperation in her voice. "Captain Donovan?"

"What can I do for you, Ma'am?"

She doesn't speak, he realizes after a moment, because she is weeping.

He lets her. Waits. Puts the pliers, grasping José's last molar, down on the ground.

"My husband had your card. He said..." More tears, throat clearing. "He said if anything happened..."

When she doesn't say anything, he says, "Something happened." José's toothless mouth tries to grin at him.

He pictures her nod, fight back tears, then, "Yes, something happened." A hoarse whisper. Just a croak.

"Who is your husband?" He knows. Just needs to

hear her say it. Say the name of the man he owes his life to.

"Chris Rogers."

Silver has to be careful not to crush the phone in his hand. "What happened?"

He pictures Rogers eating a bullet, the splatter of bone and brain and blood; or hanged, face squeezed blue, eyes bulging in a death stare; maybe a big fall off a building or cliff. Silver knew soldiers claimed by all those fates. Or pills. Or carbon monoxide.

"They killed him."

It is so unexpected, he has to sit. People aren't killed in the real world. He looks at the corpse at his feet. Not men like Rogers, shop owners. They died in their sleep, fell in the shower, a sudden heart attack.

"Who killed him?"

"One of those thugs. One of those gangsters from the neighborhood. Sons of bitches. I told him. Told him to just pay their protection money..."

"But he wouldn't."

"No sir. Said he couldn't. Couldn't do it and look at himself in the mirror. Wouldn't be able to face his son."

That's right, he had a son. That was the Chris Rogers that Silver knew, however briefly. Stubborn and brave, no matter the cost. He let out a sigh. "Mrs. Rogers, when is the service?"

"Wake'll be Wednesday. Calling hours four to eight. At Tierney's. Funeral on Thursday."

"I'll be there, Ma'am."

"Captain, you don't have to."

Yes, I do, he thinks. "I'd like to, Ma'am."

Silver pictures the pretty face on the other side of the phone, other side of the country. He checked up on Chris Rogers. A few years back. Remembers the woman at the counter of the store. A brunette with pale, porcelain skin, blue eyes, a sad smile. Remembers Rogers. Sergeant Rogers in his wheel chair. Silver watched from the street for five minutes. He wanted to go in. Talk to him. Shake his hand. Apologize again. Let Rogers take a swing at him. The sergeant did not move the entire time.

Maybe next time, Donovan told himself. If he'd learned anything in the Arabian Desert, there are no next times.

THREE

—

KATE ROGERS STANDS at the wake and begins to understand what it is to be shell-shocked. The line of mourners stretches out the door, like rubberneckers at a car crash, they look at her husband in the coffin. She accepts their sympathy, their hugs, their kisses. Numb and exhausted, the faces begin to blur. Kate has been taking her husband's anti-depression medicine and feels like she is wearing a heavy black veil over her face.

Not long ago, she had stood in the same spot as the same mourners had paid their respects to Chris's dad. They had just found out about Chris's injury. Kate knew it was the knowledge of his broken son that had done him in. She remembers it as a daze of aunts, uncles, cousins, family friends, customers; the whole neighborhood. They all knew about Chris and upon seeing Kate, their sympathy would double. "You poor dear," all the old ladies said.

Now, they say it again. But Kate picks up on the slightly different tone. The hint of relief in their voices. The common thought that, maybe, this was a mercy killing.

Part of her knows that the man she married, the man she loved, never made it back from Afghanistan. The man that came back was a mess. Would burst into sudden tears or angry tirades, over nothing. Screamed in his sleep. Their son looked at his father in terror. She was afraid to leave the boy alone with his dad.

Chris wouldn't touch her. Or let her touch him. She was lonelier than when he had been away. The heat of his body next to her in bed was a kind of torture.

A soldier stands in front of her.

She looks at his uniform, at the green beret in his hand. "Captain Donovan?"

He walks with a cane, she sees. It shines as brightly as the medals on his chest, as his eyes. "Mrs. Rogers, I'm so sorry."

He really is, she sees.

"Thank you for coming."

He looks uncomfortable. Like he's not sure whether to walk away or salute. Offers his hand.

"If you need anything..."

"Thank you."

He turns to her son, Andrew.

The boy looks up at the man in uniform. "Are you a soldier?"

Donovan smiles. He has perfect white teeth, she notices. "I was, son."

"Did you know my dad?"

Kate knows she is holding up the line but she cannot take her eyes off this man as he leans down on one knee to get face to face with her ten-year-old son.

"Andrew, right?"

"Yes."

"Andrew, your father saved my life."

Kate sees something she didn't think possible. A glimmer of pride in Andrew's eyes, in his filling lungs.

"That's how he hurt his legs. Saving me and my men. He never told you the story?"

Andrew shakes his head. Kate almost shakes her own. No, he never talked about the war.

Captain Donovan uses his cane to stand. Looks at Kate, sees her surprise. Andrew's eyes are wide. "Maybe I can tell it to you some time."

"Tomorrow?" Her son's expression is greedy.

"Maybe."

Kate looks down the line of mourners.

That son of a bitch.

Her eyelids lower, revealing only a thin strip of her poisonous green eyes. The hair on the back of her neck, like an angry dog's, rises. Everyone turns to see the squat man with the comic book super hero jaw. The air in the funeral home crackles.

The short man is the last to realize Kate's stare on him.

"Nathan Riley," she says. "Get the hell out of this line and the hell out of this building." She feels the color burning in her face.

"Just paying my respects, Kate." A tremor of emotion in his voice.

"We don't want anything of yours here." She turns back to Donovan.

"Thanks again, Captain."

Donovan puts a hand on Andrew's shoulder. "Ma'am."

FOUR

—

THAT NIGHT, DONOVAN FINDS a hotel and a bottle
of Maker's Mark. And remembers. The spirits in the
glass rile the spirits in his head. Welcome and unwel-
come ghosts join him for a drink.

After Iraq the CIA came knocking. They were looking for a liaison between agencies, the spooks and the
Rangers, and whatever other Special Forces might be
needed, SEALs, Delta Force. James Bond, Jason Bourne
stuff. Donovan was in. He traded in his desert uniform
for a suit and tie and spent some time at Langley, on
the Farm. Counter terrorism, counter insurgency.

Conspiracies were like static electricity there. The
globe, outside the borders of the United States was
infected with threats. If you weren't paranoid, you
were uninformed. India and Pakistan were about to
go nuclear. The Middle East and Africa were breeding
grounds for terrorist groups, Al Qaeda was a virus for

which there was no vaccine. North Korea was run by a mad hermit and they had the biggest standing army in the world. Donovan's old friend, Saddam, was just biding his time, building nuclear weapons underground. What else could he be doing in those bunkers? Trying to beat Iran to the punch. Donovan thought it far-fetched, knew most of those bunkers were filled with gold and other loot. Saddam's pirate booty.

Donovan wanted to talk sense to someone but sense and logic were in short supply. And he was needed in Somalia, the hot, dusty city of Mogadishu. He was there when the Black Hawk fell. Furious when American troops were pulled out. No next times.

Until another Bush made it to the White House. Then September eleventh burned a hole in the history books, in every calendar. The paranoia was back. All the way to the top of the food chain.

War with Afghanistan. Knee jerk. Foolish. Ask Alexander the great. Ask the British. Ask the Russians. Donovan was getting tired of the human price of war – on both sides. For what? What was the goal in Afghanistan? To beat the desert and mountains into submission? Blow them back to the Stone Age, some said. They were already there. To find some renegade Saudi terrorist who was probably hiding out in the lawless mountains between Afghanistan and Pakistan? Wherethfuckistan, the spooks called it. For that you didn't need to declare war.

Then Iraq. Again. Weapons of mass destruction. Bullshit. The stupidest intelligence ever gathered justified that war. Hearsay and compromised sources, none of it would have been allowed in an American court of law. But here was Colin Powell faking it at the United Nations. A sad day. Powell looked like he loathed every word that came out of his mouth. Donovan did too.

Didn't make sense. Saddam wasn't a Bond villain. He was a thug in a white suit. He didn't want to blow up the world. Just wanted to pick its pockets.

In the war rooms of Langley and DC, the electronic maps glowed red in the Middle Eastern deserts, as though they were radioactive. Donovan went back. Baghdad. Fallujah. Blood. Sand. No plutonium. Not even trace amounts. Saddam was found. Killed. America forgot why they had come. With Saddam gone, so was the threat. Right?

Kabul. Kandahar. Jalalabad. Blood. Sand. Beards. No Bin Laden. Not a trace. Afghanistan was social Darwinism put to the test. Survival of the fittest. A land of warlords. Drug dealers in turbans who controlled the poppy fields of the south. There was a simple solution which Donovan voiced in a meeting in Kabul. President Karzai sat at one end of a long, crowded table. General Patreus at the other end.

"Burn the fields," Donovan said. "We know where they are. Destroy them."

The General, chest crammed with gleaming medals

and stars, looked down at the President, resplendent in his cashmere, multi-colored Kaftan, blue and green stripes intricately threaded.

Vanity, a deadly sin, Donovan thought.

"It is not so simple." Karzai's English as elegant as his clothes.

"No?" Donovan said.

A stern glance from the General.

"No." A sterner glance from the President. "You do not realize the turmoil that would cause, the vacuum you would create."

"And the warlords who control the fields?" Patreus now. "What of them?"

"Don't be so quick to condemn them." Karzai the silver-tongued. "They were living under the Taliban. They did what they had to to survive." Sounded so sensible coming from this suave Afghan gentleman.

A smooth criminal. Donovan knew a gangster when he saw one.

Patreus was persuaded. Some of these warlords were needed to keep the peace. The drug trade should be condemned, but at times, we must look the other way. Reality had to be faced. The poverty caused by cutting off the supply of opium would drive all of southern Afghanistan back to the Taliban.

"Perhaps this is the Captain's goal?" Karzai had the lazy eyes of a serpent.

In these eyes, Donovan saw how cold-blooded the

President was. Donovan bit his tongue, swallowed his pride and gave Karzai a humble bow. "I was mistaken, Mr. President." The words tasted like chalk in his mouth. He spit them out.

Karzai was magnanimous. "It is a complicated place."

Patreus wondered aloud, "What will it take to control these men?"

Karzai's smile had no teeth. "That is simple. Cash."

American dollars. Stacks and stacks and stacks of it. To buy the warlords, to pay off the politicians, bribe the judges, consider it a capital investment for a burgeoning democracy. Think of it as securing influence, Karzai purred. It was difficult to imagine a better option than President Karzai for the United States. He saw things our way, for the most part. Didn't he? So intelligent, so enjoyable to deal with.

There was a twisted logic to his plan. Support certain sympathetic warlords. Chip away at those loyal to the Taliban.

That was where Donovan came in.

He worked with the US Army, Afghan troops and the CIA to set up sting operations. The United States military was too tempting a partner for the warlords. A new avenue to a new market. Donovan posed as a dirty soldier. A buyer. A player with access to cash. An entrepreneurial spirit without a lot of scruples. His partner in crime, an old friend from JFK school. Brian

King. King was fearless. A red-headed devil with wild eyes. BK wore a straw cowboy hat, sunglasses and a two-gun holster rig around his waist like some kind of old west gunslinger. He grew a beard and his nickname soon became Yosemite Sam. He took to quoting the old cartoon character: "Any of you lily-livered varmints care to slap leather with me?"

King was a magnet for a certain kind of attention.

They caught a few small fish.

Donovan remembers a dark, quiet alley in a dark, quiet corner of Kandahar. Or were he and King lured there? A small, rat infested apartment. The man they were targeting began to shout at them. Donovan understood just enough to know he was being called a dog. The rest was all vitriol spewing from the man's face. He remembers the barrel of the man's Kalashnikov pulling his eyes to it. A shot made Donovan jump out of his skin, but it was King's pistol, firing a bullet into the Afghan's skull.

"My spider sense was tingling," King said.

Donovan fell to his knees, shaken.

A firefight erupted. The Afghans waiting outside with the drugs panicked. Where was their leader? What was that gunshot? King, asshole, pushed their leader's limp body out the door. He thought it might break their spirits. A swarm of bullets crashed through the boarded up windows.

"If you hadn't just saved my life, King, I'd chuck you out after him."

King flashed his crooked teeth. They were both still young back then, still invincible. Bullet proof.

Donovan called in for reinforcements. "Wait, King," he called as the young cowboy bolted out the door, dodging bullets and returning fire.

The cavalry arrived. The drugs were confiscated, the Afghans arrested.

It was a slow, dangerous way to go about it. At this rate, the allied troops would be long gone before any real progress was made. This was probably Karzai's secret hope.

Donovan decided to aim higher. Catch a bigger fish. He went through channels. Patreus and the CIA signed off on it. A big buy would have to go successfully. Reel them in, document it. Then a bigger buy. That was the plan. The last approval was Karzai.

The President listened. He wasn't wearing his usual Karakul hat and his bald head gleamed. Inside, wheels turned, calculations were made. He squinted at Donovan. "Good luck, Captain." The light was green.

Donovan handpicked his team. King, of course.

Also Chris Burns, their wheelman. He could drive, fly or sail any vehicle known to man. Nickname: Crash. Five feet, eight inches of solid muscle.

Billy, don't call me Willie, Nelson. Billy and Donovan had gone through basic training together, had both been selected for the Rangers. By now they could almost communicate telepathically. Invaluable in combat.

And Doc. An ROTC kid. Four years of service, then medical school. After 9/11, he re-upped. He was as good at killing bad guys as he was at saving good guys.

Their superiors referred to them as the Fab Five.

They found their big fish.

A man in Kandahar who knew about such things, who connected buyers and sellers, set it up.

Donovan and Billy met the seller in a cafe. The old man who set it up acted as translator.

The warlord looked the part. Tan robes and a turban wrapped around a rugged, scarred face. Deep voice.

"He asks," the translator said, "where does the money come from?"

"For building schools." Donovan leered. "For women and girls."

The old man translated.

The warlord slapped each of them on the back.

Tomorrow, it was decided, at night, at the edge of town. Bring the money. Everything seemed good. Donovan sent it up the flag pole and it flew by his superiors.

It was cold that night. Their breath mixed with the engine exhaust beneath a crescent moon. Kandahar's million residents slept. They loaded the opium into a van while the warlord counted the money.

"Is there more where this came from?" He spoke English.

Donovan pointed to the drugs. "Is there more where that came from?"

The warlord found this hilarious. He had one of his men take the money away. Still laughing, he pulled a nickel plated .45 caliber Smith & Wesson out of its holster and shot King in the head.

Donovan's hand, always cool, always calm, shook with rage as he fired at the warlord, missing twice.

The tribesmen were gone in seconds.

"Do we follow?" Billy Nelson asked.

Donovan shook his head. Not tonight. Soon.

The expression on King's dead face. Like he was about to tell the funniest joke he'd ever heard.

This was when Donovan learned the healing properties of alcohol. Whiskey could bring down a curtain between the drinker and the world, between a man and his troubles. Jameson's could make it hard to remember. Donovan climbed into a bottle. Lost track of the days. Sometimes his memory got so bad, he forgot King was dead. Thought King was in the room with him. They had long conversations about King's childhood in California. He'd grown up in San Diego. A surfer kid.

"Christ, Kinger , I forgot."

"What?"

"You're dead, man. Stop talking to me."

King shrugged. "Stop talking to me."

"Good point."

It must have been early. Donovan could see sun through the cracks in the window blinds. Dust motes danced in the air.

"I'm sorry, King. I should have seen it coming."

"Shit, I should have seen it."

Donovan broke the seal on another bottle. After another few sips, King came back into focus while the room around them got blurry. "It was a set up. Had to be."

"Makes sense. But who?"

"Only one way to know for sure."

King grinned and blood seeped out of the wound in his head, then out of his mouth. "Two things." He held up one finger. "Sober up." He held up the second finger. "Make it hurt."

When Donovan woke up, he felt like a crash landed space alien with no concept of the time of day or year or the local language, lost in the universe. He concentrated on the simple things. Standing, walking out of the room.

Billy Nelson sat in the living room in a rickety wicker chair, reading a paper. "Welcome back."

They had waited in shifts for Donovan to snap out of it. Going back to base to cover for him, to sneak booze back. They'd been busy. Finding the location of King's murderer.

Donovan drank strong tea, ate lamb kabobs, and slowly started to feel human again. "Where is he?"

Crash: "In the mountains. We'll never get him there."

Doc: "He comes into the city once a month, looking to unload some product."

Nelson, Crash and Doc grinned.

Nelson: "He's got some piece of tail he bangs in the city."

"So we sit on her place?" Donovan's mind was starting to operate properly.

Crash: "No, it's no good. Just an alley really. Apartments stacked right on top of each other. Nowhere for us, Americans, to set up surveillance."

"I'm sure you geniuses have figured out a way around this."

More grins.

Nelson: "The downstairs neighbor."

"Seriously?"

Nelson: "She's just an Allah fearing old widow. Thinks the mistress's behavior is scandalous."

"So we've got some old lady spying for us?"

Doc held up two fingers.

"Two old ladies?"

Doc: "She's got a sister. They're working in shifts. One day, one night. According to our translator, they don't sleep much anyway."

"You fucking guys."

Nelson: "The nosy sisters tip us off. We catch him as he leaves. Pick our spot, take him out."

"Nope." Donovan paused until he had all their attention. "We have a chat with him first. I want to know who tipped him off."

They didn't love the idea.

Doc: "Risky."

Crash: "Time consuming."

Nelson: "We're going beyond an eye for an eye, here."

"Way beyond. And I'd do the same for any of you and you know it."

They knew it.

The four of them waited. Three weeks. No word. They ran the occasional mission. Crash got a nice scar on his face from a roadside bomb. Maiwand District was like a well-tended garden of IED's. Things could always be worse, could always be better. That was life in Afghanistan.

Word came from Kabul. Another attempt on Karzai's life. A suicide bomber. Donovan could read the writing on the wall. His team would be redeployed soon. They needed to get this done.

Finally, the call came. Dusk. Evening prayers were just beginning.

Crash had requisitioned a Humvee from the motor pool, removed the US flag logos. Still conspicuous but difficult to identify. Similar to what some of the warlords drove. With luck, their actions would be mis-interpreted as a turf war.

They rumbled through the narrow streets of the city. Donovan often wondered if colors, other than brown and white, had been outlawed in Afghanistan. Everything was the color of sand or snow or stone, even the people. It was the drabbest place he'd ever been. The only bright colors, the blue sky and the blood of soldiers.

Dim light in the mistress's apartment. They waited down the street. A brighter light in the sisters' apart-ment underneath. To calm their nerves, a flask was passed from man to man. Dusk darkened to night. The lights in the apartments grew brighter. Silhouettes moved in the apartment above.

Two black Toyota Land Cruisers loitered at the curb in front of the woman's apartment building. Donovan counted six men. All with rifles over their shoulders, they smoked and joked with criminal swaggers. These were battle tested killers.

Donovan smiled. So were they.

He and his men were in full riot gear. Body armor, helmets, balaclavas, they looked like Darth Vader without the cape. May the force be with them.

Before long, the warlord came out. Knowing glances were exchanged between him and his men.

Crash adjusted his grip on the steering wheel. All of them took a collective deep breath. Donovan and his men understood the rush that came in the small, quiet moments before battle, welcomed it, lived for it. They felt connected at these times with an unending history of warriors; gladiators waiting beneath the coliseum; Leonidas' three hundred at Thermopylae; Alexander's cavalry. They might be waiting on the very ground that Bucephalus galloped on. It was in these minutes that a soldier's soul was forged, or shattered, by the god of war's hammer.

Donovan observed his fellows. Eyes hard and flat and mean. A flutter of pride in his chest. They were birds of prey circling. When the Afghan men were in their vehicles, he said, "Go time."

Crash floored it.

The Humvee roared across the street, slammed into the front vehicle, pushing, groaning until the Toyota was on its side. The undercarriage gleamed in the high beams.

Crash and Donovan out the left side.

Doc and Nelson out the right.

Fourth of July. A riot of bullets hit metal and flesh, asphalt and cement. The Americans hit like a lightning strike, rolled like thunder.

The stunned warlord was on his back on a pile of broken glass inside the Land Cruiser. Donovan watched him gather his wits, look at his dead friends, reach for his pistol.

"No," Donovan said.

The man looked at the Americans with rabid eyes. Donovan wouldn't have been surprised to see him foam at the mouth.

Then Crash yanked him through the shattered windshield. He wasn't gentle. The warlord hissed Persian curses through yellow teeth, they sounded like wicked enchantments.

Doc and Nelson were there. Nelson tied the warlord's hands behind him.

Donovan stepped close. Removed his balaclava.

Recognition leaked through the warlord's fury. Maybe fear. Maybe.

"Remember me?" Donovan hit him on the bridge of the nose before he had a chance to spit at him.

They packed him into the back of the Humvee.

As Crash backed up and pulled away, Donovan looked at his watch. Three minutes. A well-oiled machine.

Doc administered a sedative to the warlord, then taped his mouth shut. Taped his legs together. Covered him in military equipment and a tarp.

Crash drove north on the Kandahar Kabul Highway. Donovan's credentials got them through most of the checkpoints with a quick salute.

"All eyes, Captain," a sergeant said. "Some action downtown."

"Will do, Sarge. You watch yourself."

The sergeant glanced at the damage to the front of

the Humvee. They held their breaths until he waved them through.

It was a desolate road, flanked by squat buildings. Beyond, snowcapped mountain ranges held up the sky. The adrenaline faded. Donovan yawned.

"You got your kit, Doc?"

Doc touched his little black bag. Sodium pentothal. *Here's hoping that does it*, Donovan thought.

On a long, dark stretch of highway with no buildings, they took a right off the road, going by compass now, Crash turned off the headlights. The moon was just enough to see by. Nothing to look at but sand anyway. The mountains grew, taller and closer, they reached the foothills, found the markers they'd left for their abandoned cave. A primitive interrogation room.

The warlord was awake now. Good. They carried him past the ditch they had dug for his corpse. Let him see how far from hope he was. Inside, a chair, some candles. Crash and Nelson tied him to the chair. He didn't cooperate. They were happy to make him.

Donovan stood in front of him. Stared him down. For five minutes. Didn't move, didn't speak. Then he tore the tape off the warlord's mouth.

The warlord howled, threatened all of them in a language they didn't understand. Tried to bust out of his restraints, managed to topple over on his side. More howls.

Donovan watched. Didn't move. Didn't speak. Waited until the man screamed himself hoarse.

Then he sighed. "Your name is Abdul Khan."

Abdul Khan looked confused.

"You are a member of the Kharoti tribe. Educated in Islamabad." Donovan crouched. "Where you studied, among other things, English."

Abdul Khan closed his eyes.

"I need one thing. One name." Donovan's finger cast a shadow over Khan's face.

Doc opened his black bag, made a show of pulling the syringe out. The smell of alcohol invaded the cold cave. Khan shivered.

"Who told you?" Donovan said.

Eyes locked on Doc, Abdul Khan said, "Karzai."

Donovan looked at the others, took in their surprise. "President Karzai?" It made sense. The President had known about their operation. Had demanded final approval.

The warlord chuckled. "Ahmed Wali Karzai."

Ah. The President's half-brother. The King of Kandahar, they called him. Drug kingpin. *Dead man walking*, Donovan thought.

Doc looked disappointed. "That's it? Don't get to use any of my toys?"

Nelson stepped close to Khan. Removed a nasty looking knife from his utility belt. They had drawn straws for the duty. The honor of avenging King.

"Be quick," Donovan said and left.

"But not too quick," Crash said on his way out.

When they got back to the highway, a sharp eye could just make out the flickering light at the foot of the mountain from where they had torched their interrogation cave. They paid no attention. The wheels in their heads were already turning, moving ahead to the next target.

They ditched the Humvee, in a garage in Kandahar. It was prearranged, no questions asked. Traded for a cheap sedan. Everybody wins. Before long, they were back in their barracks. The sky was turning blue. It only took a night.

A man in a tan suit waited for them. Donovan had seen him before. Even if he hadn't, he would have known the man was CIA, a spook.

"Captain Donovan."

"Agent Henry. Is that your first or last name?"

Henry smiled. "Just Henry. Like Prince."

"What can we do for you, Prince Henry?"

A bigger smile. "Lieutenant Burns, you can take your hand off your pistol."

Crash kept his hand where it was.

Henry shrugged. "You think I'd come to arrest four renegade Special Forces soldiers solo?"

Crash: "Maybe."

Henry: "I'm good. I'm not that good. Or that dumb."

"So what's this about?" Donovan motioned for Crash to cool it.

Crash put his hands by his sides.

"I think you guys took out Abdul Khan tonight." Henry held up his hands. "I'm sure there's nothing to link you guys to it. Besides your whereabouts not being accounted for. I'm impressed. *We're* impressed." The royal we. Not just him. The CIA. "But maybe you're not done. Maybe you just needed a name. Am I close?"

Poker faces all around.

"Maybe the name he provided was the same as the President's."

Doc: "Enough maybes."

Henry: "Okay. It was. And you tough guys are going after Karzai's brother. And I want to help. *We* want to help."

Donovan asked the obvious question. "Why?"

Henry explained how Patreus and President Karzai were tight. They went way back, to the Soviet occupation. But there was another side. Henry enlightened them. Not everyone was thrilled with the present situation. The CIA was looking for a well-trained, highly motivated team that could be trusted to keep their mouths shut.

"Know anybody who might fit the bill?"

They just might.

Donovan asked the other obvious question: "What's the catch?"

"There will be another mission, after this one is completed."

They could live with it. To avenge King, it was worth it. They didn't need to consult each other. They all nodded at the same time.

"Excellent. I've got some paperwork y'all should study." He pulled what looked like blueprints out of a long canister.

Doc: "What's that?"

Henry unrolled the paper. "The plans to Karzai's compound."

Fortress was more like it. Impenetrable at first glance, second glance and last glance. A labyrinth of walls and barbed wire and gates. Invisible in the plans were the armed guards stationed every fifty feet.

Nelson: "Where'd you get this?"

Henry: "We built it for him."

Doc made a clicking noise with his tongue.

"What's up, Doc?" Donovan said.

"Ever see Star Wars?"

They nodded.

"The Death Star?"

Crash: "What are you getting at?"

"This thing's made to stop suicide bombers. Or a platoon of Taliban soldiers. He's thinking big, but he's not thinking small."

Okay," Donovan said. "A small team. At night?"

"Probably. We'll have to monitor him for a while."

"We can provide some intel there," Henry said. "He's been under light surveillance for over a year."

Light surveillance. Satellite views. Film from across the street revealed guard numbers, shift changes. Blind spots could be located.

The blueprints revealed formidable defenses around Karzai's living quarters. But above was thin. After a week of study and planning they told Henry they had a way in.

Henry had been busy. The CIA was all about covering their tracks. He'd approached Wali Karzai's trusted bodyguard, Sarder Mohammed, about working for the CIA. They needed him to pose as a man disillusioned by his boss, a man who missed the days of Taliban rule. Mohammed could not turn down the money. Meetings were set up, unbeknownst to Wali Karzai. In meetings with the Taliban, the question was asked, *Would Mohammed be willing to murder his boss, for the good of Afghanistan?* It did not sit well with Mohammed, this double speak. He was not a natural spy. He couldn't sleep. He bickered with his fellow bodyguards.

Just before dawn, they scaled the walls of Wali Karzai's compound. Donovan, Nelson, Crash and Doc. In a small, private office, they waited.

Henry gave Mohammed information about a Taliban assassination attempt. He impressed upon his new agent that time was wasting, he should immediately tell Wali Karzai. "Go to his compound, but talk to him in private. Trust nobody."

Donovan listened to the hushed voices of Wali Karzai and Mohammed as they stepped into the private office. Mohammed held a folder. He handed it to his boss.

Donovan pounced, grabbed Mohammed's pistol out of its holster and fired twice at Wali Karzai's head.

Mohammed's eyes wide with shock and terror.

Donovan threw Mohammed's pistol back to him. Mohammed caught it and fired a second after Nelson shot him with a silenced Beretta, making Mohammed's shot go wild and hit Wali Karzai in the hand.

They escaped through an air vent, crawling like rats through tunnels.

Behind them an arsenal unloaded bullets into the shocked body of Sarder Mohammed. The murderer found, there was no reason to hunt for anyone else.

Quick and clean and cruel. A perfect operation.

Donovan had to admit, it felt good taking Wali Karzai out. That made it easier to forget the look on the betrayed bodyguard's face. They laid low in a small CIA safe house nearby until the hubbub died down. Hours later, they drove back to base. Henry congratulated them, pointed to the television. Al Jazeera showed images of Sarder Mohammed's body, with more bullets than blood in it, being strung up in the central square of the market downtown.

Quick and clean and cruel.

"Nice work, boys," Henry said. "Rest up. Have a nice meal. Tomorrow at breakfast, we'll talk about the next target."

The mob at the market was throwing stones at the dead body. Every one of them meant for Donovan.

In his dreams, the corpses of Brian King and Sarder Mohammed argued about ends and means. And justice. Their bodies were pocked with wounds, they looked like they'd died of bubonic plague.

"We are all just little people." King's jaw is stiff from rigor mortis. "Caught up in history. In events much larger than us."

"No," Mohammed said. "We are all holy creatures. All our lives are sacred."

King sneered as well as he could with his dead face. "You think we're all equal, Punjab?"

"Yes."

"Take a look around, jackass. Allah doesn't care anymore than God about ninety-nine percent of his people. They both just hang us all out to dry."

"Do you believe that, King?" Donovan said.

King straightened out his moustache, an absurd gesture on his ruined face. "I do now, Captain. Course I got all the answers now. Like having the answer key. Trust me, you and the boys got a lot to figure out. But don't worry. You will."

King's growl haunted him all morning.

The four of them ate breakfast in silence. They had learned not to ask about each other's dreams. Henry plopped a newspaper down on the table they were sitting at. A picture of Ahmed Wali Karzai. Donovan was certain the word above the picture in large, bold print was: *Murdered*. Henry tapped the picture next to him, a somber President Karzai.

Suddenly they were not hungry.

President Karzai.

Henry spoke. "How do you think his brother found out? Where do you think these warlords come from? Most of 'em are Mujahidin. We trained them, we armed them. Same as Karzai.

Donovan wondered, not for the first time, if anything mattered in this broken city, this broken country, this broken world. What would it matter if he took a broken shard of it and broke it some more?

Next month, Henry informed them, the President would be giving a speech. Big crowds, lots of opportunities.

For four weeks, they planned. They practiced, taking note of the angle of the sun at the time of the speech. They set up a life size model of the venue miles north of the city in the foothills of the Kush Mountains. Donovan, the shooter, aimed at a scarecrow Karzai, with a melon for a head. Again and again, it exploded.

The speech was delayed. Several hours.

Donovan's team did not look out of place, they just looked like extra security. They set up where they had rehearsed, a flat patio off a fourth floor apartment in back of the crowd.

President Karzai was introduced to cheers from the crowd.

They had to be fast.

But the delay changed the position of the sun. Donovan realized a moment too late.

The scope lens reflected the light, caught the attention of one of Karzai's men. He watched Donovan take aim at his President. The Afghan soldier pointed his rifle at the American.

The next domino to fall was a US Army sergeant, Chris Rogers, who saw a local soldier about to shoot an American soldier. Sergeant Rogers did not hesitate but shot the Afghan soldier four times.

Chaos.

President Karzai was evacuated, like a magic trick he vanished.

The Afghan soldier's shots were altered by the bullets ripping into him. Rather than hitting Donovan in the chest, where he was aiming, the shots tore through the Captain's foot, shredding skin and muscle and bone. A festival of pain. He dropped to his knees.

Chris Rogers was shot eight times. One bullet made a permanent home in his spine. He would never walk again.

The last thing Donovan would see, before the flames of his own pain consumed him, was Chris Rogers dragging himself next to a young girl, ten maybe, whose clothes were quickly turning crimson from the wounds she'd received. Sergeant Rogers held her hand, whispered in her ear.

Yes, she is the last phantom sent to haunt Donovan, to wake him from his dreams. She stands before him, her drab perahaan dress stained scarlet. Slowly, she unwraps it from her thin, ten-year-old body, a body just at the bud of womanhood. Puckered with bullet wounds oozing blood.

He wakes covering his eyes but only sees more clearly.

Her face is different every time. The only thing that doesn't change is her eyes, the only thing he ever actually saw of her. He feels them burn the back of his skull, those eyes.

He thinks they will be here today. Doc, Nelson, Crash.

Doc had a hand in saving Donovan's life that day in Kandahar. The bastard. The three of them had dragged and carried Donovan out of the crowd. Doc reluctantly applied the tourniquet. Not much foot left to save anyway and the wound pumped blood like jelly.

Now Doc is a surgeon at Yale/New Haven Hospital. Not too far a drive for him.

A few years back, Donovan had been in a jam. Some

trouble in New York. Another bullet with Donovan's name on it. Doc was married by then, maybe a kid, Donovan couldn't remember—Afghanistan was a long time ago. But he'd come through. Gave Donovan directions to his office at two in the morning. Removed the bullet, stitched him up.

They didn't ask about each other's lives. Everything they needed to know was in that room. Donovan's wound, the .32 with a silencer in a shoulder holster. Doc's office, the pictures of his family in the lobby. Instead they traded awkward silences.

"Stay out of trouble, Donovan."

"It has a way of tracking me down."

"Yes it does. It always did." Doc's hair was starting to gray. Just a touch of paunch, the beginnings of jowls on his face. Doc handed Donovan a card. "For the next time."

Doc was comfortably numb–he was always comfortably numb these days – when Donovan called.

"What can I do for you, Captain?"

"At ease, Lieutenant. You remember that kid, Chris Rogers? From the Karzai mission?"

Donovan waited for Doc to digest the question. Let his brain recover from the memories he would have to sift through.

"The one who saved our asses?"

"He was killed a few days ago."

"Killed?"

Doc was surprised how much it hurt, what Donovan was telling him. Shocked at how angry it made him.

"Funeral's tomorrow. Just wanted you to know."

"Give me the address."

But in the meantime, a little something to get him on a different planet, to heal these reopened scabs, or at least not feel them bleeding. Now that his wife and kid were gone, for good apparently, he didn't have to worry about keeping up appearances. He tied off his arm, found a pretty blue vein, shot a warm surge of bliss up his arm. As the fuzzy glow worked through his system, he dug out his old uniform.

Billy Nelson owns a bar in west Texas, not far from El Paso, not far from the border. Dim and dusty, he is an imposing sight behind the counter, dark hair gone silver at the temples still high and tight, a scowl on his mouth and a squint in his eye greets every patron. From the jukebox, Willie Nelson, Waylon Jennings, Emmylou Harris, Loretta Lynn croon about good hearted women and good timing men.

Now and then a stranger will enter and belly up to the bar and order a sarsaparilla. Billy will open a bottle, pour it and walk to the back room. The stranger, after a sip of soda, will follow. It is an open secret that Billy is an arms dealer, uses his military contacts to outfit cartels on both sides of the border.

The regulars are smart enough not to ask about the

strangers. Billy is smart enough not to talk to them about it.

It is not unusual to hear from his old captain, who sends an occasional client his way. Billy remembers the man, Chris Rogers. Remembers the mission gone sideways in Afghanistan. Remembers the man, just a boy really, floating on a drug induced cloud in the GI hospital in Berlin. The guilt that always lurks just beneath the surface comes bubbling up into his heart. He'll be there.

Crash got out of the army a year after Donovan. None of them were the same after that failed mission. Before that, they'd been invincible, bullet-proof. Fear was always part of the equation. You knew what you were risking, this was life or death, but Crash hadn't thought about going through life injured. He'd rather take one to the head than one to the spine. When you started to think like that, started to do that math, it slowed you down, just a half a step, but half a step was too much when the guys you were up against had no second thoughts, no hesitation – just like you used to.

He's a fireman now. Chris Burns, the fireman, his buddies get a kick out of that one. Nobody calls him Crash anymore. Just Burns, or Burnsy. He runs into burning buildings. He carries people out. Sprays water on four alarm fires. And he gets to drive the ladder truck. That's his favorite, hauling ass in that long red blur, siren wailing, lights flashing, steering wheel as big as a ship's, slicing through the city streets. This is his life now. Nobody shots at him, he doesn't shoot at anybody. But he still gets to risk his life. It's enough. Isn't it?

He tells himself this is his penance. A life saved for every life he took. Does that balance the books?

Then the Captain calls.

What a fucking shame. Dead? Shot? God. Damn. See you there, Cap.

Crash thinks about the last time he saw Sergeant Rogers.

Donovan had insisted, once he was able to walk again, on visiting Chris Rogers. The sergeant was convalescing in Germany. He was in a heap of trouble because Donovan and his team were not there, officially. So, officially, Rogers had opened fire on a member of the Afghan Special Police with no provocation. He was looking at a dishonorable discharge, as soon as he was healthy enough to stand trial.

Donovan was furious.

Agent Henry was adamant. "You boys were never there. You weren't even in Kandahar that day, you were in Kabul. If you mess with my version of events," his eyes smoldered, "I will cut you guys loose and feed you to the Afghanistan army."

"And that kid?"

"You think I'm happy about this? It's war. There are casualties. This is not news. You want fair, go play football. They've got three refs and instant replay." Henry stopped himself. Face red, fists clenched, he closed his eyes and forced himself to relax. "If it makes you feel any better, I'm sure the Devil's got a chair all warmed up for me in hell."

"Where is he?"

"Who?"

"Rogers."

Henry's eyes were stone. So were Donovan's.

Henry blinked. "Berlin. Don't make me do something we're all going to regret."

"How is he?" Donovan knew the answer. Wanted Henry to have to say it.

"He's a mess."

FIVE

—

SERGEANT ROGERS, more science project than man, lay in a hospital bed. A medical experiment of tubes and gauze and plaster, the smell of alcohol, the beeps of electronic equipment, the hushed whispers of nurses and doctors with their occasional questions. *Can you feel this, Sergeant Rogers?* He never can. Rogers was on something to numb the pain, but he still knew things were bad. Very bad. Lucid moments came to him rarely. Consciousness was fleeting, too painful.

A dark high tide of morphine would always claim him.

She watched after him there.

The girl who died.

He remembered, he thought he remembered, removing her head wrap. Rogers wanted to see her face. So young. The force of her hand squeezing his, how hard she tried to hold on to life. He was grateful for her robes, covering the wounds staining the beige fabric. Stains that would never come out. His own pain overwhelmed him, but he knew she was hurt worse, knew every breath could be her last. The terror and pain in her eyes, he wanted to chase it away. He thought of his son, breaking his arm sledding. The song his wife used to soothe him came into his head.

Black bird singing in the dead of night
Take these broken wings and learn to fly
All your life
You were only waiting for this moment to arrive

Was it possible, in the din surrounding them, that she heard him? That his song provided some comfort? By the time he'd finished the verse, her eyes were as empty as the sky above them. What was her name?

He wept.

But she was there now. His black bird in the dead of night. Somehow there in the hospital. A song on her lips. A foreign lullaby. A ghostly nightingale's wale.

She never spoke, only sang, or hummed. Her fingers on his forehead cold as death but they soothed his fever. Her wounds were healed, the terror in her face replaced with concern, the fear there now only for him. Could she take him with her? To the place where wounds are healed. Knowing his thoughts, she shook her head. Not yet.

But it hurts.

She knew, she knew all about hurt.

Rogers opened his eyes, or thought he did.

A man in a chair. His right hand rested on a cane. He was familiar. A captain's uniform, a green beret in his lap. The Afghan soldier's target.

The pain returned, like a black liquid, the ocean at night. Blackness drowned him.

The man was still there when the pain subsided. Sitting. Patient. Rogers saw three others. More green berets. One he recognized, the other two were strangers. But they must have been there too, he figured.

"Sergeant, I'm Captain Patrick Donovan."

Spoken words were chewy in the sergeant's drug addled head. Hard to hold onto. Slippery on his lips. He stammered in response.

The man Donovan put up his hand. "Easy, soldier. You're in a bad way." He took a deep breath. "And I'm afraid we put you there."

Rogers shook his head. Confusion like tiny spiders loose in his brain.

"But they'll never admit it." The officer held out a card. "I'm going to put this in your locker. You get into trouble, any kind, you call this number. I'll do what I can."

Rogers hadn't concentrated this long since he was injured. The pain and the morphine reclaimed him.

The four men were gone when he came to. Were they real?

His father came to visit him, in his dreams. The girl seemed to like the old man, who seemed younger now than the last time Rogers saw him. A veteran of Vietnam, his father. Came home without a scratch. He inspected his son's wounds, like he did most things, quiet and serious. Were there tears in his eyes? His father felt helpless before his wounded boy.

Rogers remembered the feeling, back in Kandahar, watching the girl's eyes harden to marbles.

"It's okay, Dad."

His father shook his head.

The little girl pulled at his old man's hand, speaking in her warbling bird call language. His father nodded, he seemed to understand. He patted her head.

His voice was thick with emotion. "She says you were very brave. Says you saved lives by taking one. She knows you were trying to comfort her with your song. That's what she's been trying to do."

A man came to tell Rogers that he was technically a prisoner in his hospital room. Charged with conduct unbecoming, manslaughter. No witnesses corroborated his story. "You need a lawyer."

"Are you a lawyer?"

"Yes."

"My lawyer?"

"Yes."

"Okay."

The attorney was no more than a boy. Like Rogers. But he seemed bright, trustworthy. Rogers would take his chances with him.

"You're in a lot of trouble," the lawyer said. "But that's not the worst of it."

His father. His father had died. "Can I talk to my wife?"

"Of course."

Her voice made everything better and everything worse. It soothed him at the same time as it reminded him of every wound. He didn't want her to see him like this, but he knew he wouldn't be looking better any time soon.

"Baby? Baby are you okay? Talk to me, Christopher."

Her voice, even filtered through God knew how many phone lines, bounced off satellites in space, was still so real he almost couldn't bear it. Realer than the ghosts that had visited him the past week or so.

"Chris?"

"I'm here, honey." Here. About as far from there as a man could be. He was grateful for the distance. Grateful that she didn't know how bad it was. Yet.

"They told us you were hurt pretty bad."

"Yup."

"A man of few words, Chris Rogers."

"Stop. It hurts to laugh." The sweetest pain he ever felt. His ribs stabbed at his sides like knives.

They laughed. They cried.

"You heard about your dad?"

"Yeah."

"The hits just keep on coming."

"Yeah. How's the boy?"

"He's a handful, just like his Daddy."

Myriad activities occurred to Rogers that he would never be able to do with his son. Going to the beach. Pushing him on a swing, taking him camping. He fought the tears but the tears won.

"So it's bad?"

"It's bad."

"I can handle bad. We can handle bad. You just get back home to us. To me."

"Okay."

"Okay then."

The kid lawyer was surprised by how cooperative the prosecuting attorney was. They'd give him an honorable discharge, as long as he pleaded guilty to the charge of conduct unbecoming.

"You have to take this deal, Chris. You don't want to mess with your pension or benefits."

"But that isn't what happened." Chris followed the pacing lawyer with his eyes, he couldn't even swivel his neck.

"Who cares?"

"American soldiers were being fire on. I stopped the gunman."

"And you want a medal? Look, I believe you. They

don't want you in a courtroom on record saying what you're saying to me. You got in the middle of something nobody wants to talk about. If you make push come to shove, The U.S. Government could make things very difficult for you. And your wife. And your kid."

"I'll take the deal."

He took some comfort in being a pawn in a vast government conspiracy. Sometimes he even believed it.

The bullet that had ruined his legs remained embedded in his spine, a grim souvenir. To remove it could do more harm than good. He was warned that the bullet might occasionally shift position and cause severe pain.

His wheelchair parked in the back of a van, Rogers was driven to the airport. Berlin startled him. The tall, old buildings, pedestrians in suits, he hadn't seen women's hair in ages. He ached to put his hands through the soft, blonde curls of those *fraus* and *frauleins*. He was glad to be moving but dreaded his destination.

Somewhere over the Atlantic, looking down through the layers of clouds, he remembered the only way into the apartment in the back of the store, a narrow, cement staircase. How could this have only just occurred to him?

The plane landed at JFK. Kate, he would find out later, bought a cheap ticket to Philadelphia so she could meet him as he came off the plane, out of the gate.

Man, how had he forgotten? That feeling, the same old tightness in his chest when he saw her, hair a little shorter, face a little thinner. She wore—on purpose?— the same clothes she'd said goodbye to him in. As though she'd never changed clothes, never left the airport, just waited for him to return. Tears in her eyes, like the last time he'd seen her. Maybe she never stopped crying.

"Christopher." In her mouth it was a magic spell.

Only when he tried to say her name did he realize how hard he was crying.

She said his name again as she hugged him, kissed his face. Christ, the smell of her. He hugged her back, fiercely, then winced as the bullet in his spine sent a shot of pain through his body, taking his breath away.

"Did I hurt you?"

He closed his eyes, to block out the pain, to erase the sight of horror and guilt in her expression. "It's okay."

But it wasn't. From then on, she touched him like he was made of glass. Like she was made of fire.

At baggage claim, Kate struggled with his enormous duffel bag. A man helped her. Tall, in a suit, he saw the situation and gallantly insisted on taking the bag to their car.

"Happy to help a veteran out." The man's

Massachusetts accent was slight. Newton or Cambridge. Educated.

Their truck, an old, blue Ford F-150, was parked in a handicapped space not far away. The man asked questions: Where you coming back from? How long you been gone? Rogers answered with as few words as possible. It cheered him up to imagine this man dying in various ways, a bullet to the head, Chris's hands around his windpipe. He got lost in these fantasies, maybe a knife severing the carotid artery. He was picturing the spray of blood when Kate's voice pulled him out of it.

"No thank you, sir. I think we'll manage. Thanks for the help."

Rogers realized that the man had asked if they needed a hand getting him inside. Chris made the man's imagined deaths more gruesome.

"Happy to be of service." He paused for an awkward moment. "Take care, soldier. Ma'am."

"Thanks." The word tasted sour on his lips.

When the man was out of earshot, Kate said, "Okay, soldier." Mocking the man's Kennedy accent. "Let's get you up in that cab."

It was a bit of a production. By straining, he could pull himself up but his legs dragged and Kate had to guide them in. He was exhausted when they were done. Kate buckled him in, like he was a child.

Once they escaped the choked streets of New York

City, onto the New York Thruway, Chris remembered that it was May. The highway was bordered by a green he had almost forgotten existed. A green that told him he was home. They passed baseball diamonds peopled with little leaguers in their still bright, early season uniforms, evoking memories of childhood.

Little league. Chris remembered Nate Riley. There was something wrong with his back as a kid, he had to wear a brace and it made him scuttle like a crab. But he could hit the hell out of the ball, two homers his first two at bats, Chris's team had to wait while he gimped around the bases, the sound of his steps on the dirt was all that could be heard after the cheers stopped. His third time up, just a dribbler to first base, to Chris. Chris waited. Could have run up and tagged him out. Could have stepped on the bag. Instead, he waited for Nate to get to his glove. Then Nate took a swing at him. Wore that red-faced, squinty-eyed look Chris would come to know so well. Caught Chris right above his left eye.

Chris touched the scar where the skin had been split.

Their fathers, both big guys, two grown up school yard bullies, broke up the fight. Made them apologize. Shake hands. Nate looked like a baby-faced gangster. What he would grow up to be. Chris had to go to the hospital for stitches.

That was the start of the feud.

If not for that, who knows? Would Chris have rushed so fast after Kate if he hadn't noticed her smiling at his pint-sized nemesis? Would he have noticed her smile at all if it hadn't been aimed at Nate? Chris liked to think so. But he couldn't deny that things between Chris and Kate had started largely out of spite. Something he would never admit to anyone. Barely admitted to himself.

They drove through Fairfield County on I84. Dogwoods in bloom barked their red and pink and white blossoms. Felt strange being a passenger. In the past, Kate never drove when they went anywhere.

"You ever see Nate Riley?"

Her hands tightened around the steering wheel, her jaw went rigid. She took a deep breath, as though a long speech was coming but then said simply, "He's around."

Chris gave her a moment to expand. She merely stewed in private with her thoughts. He was reluctant to open the door to that conversation, afraid what might come out.

Connecticut rolled past, gentle hills and valleys all painted the first green of spring. In his head, Chris listened to the buzzing of bees, breathed the smell of mowed lawns, envisioned the glistening of spider silk in the sun – landscapes so drenched in color he felt like Judy Garland as Dorothy stepping out of her house into the glorious Technicolor of Oz.

It used to be his father's job to pick Chris up when he came home from the service. He always quoted the same line from Frost, "Home again, home again, jiggedy jig."

A voice he would never hear again. The absence of it choked him. One more never. They were piling up. He was tired of the multitude of things that were gone from his life. He was tired. Sleep claimed him.

He didn't realize he was asleep. In his dream, Kate still drove him but they were in an army Humvee now, in Afghanistan, outside of Kabul.

"What are we doing here?" he said.

"What do you mean?"

"What are you doing here?"

"Taking you home, Christopher."

"But I don't live here."

"Sure you do."

There was no warning. There never was with a roadside bomb. The front driver side of the vehicle erupted with fire and shattered metal and Kate was gone, then Chris was thrown from the truck, landed on his back, legs useless. The girl is there. Of course. Bleeding. Dying.

He screamed himself awake.

Kate kept her voice calm. "It's okay, Christopher. We're home."

Seemed different. Like his house in his dreams was different, but he couldn't place why. A bubbling anxiety in his chest made him reach for his blue pills. He was supposed to take two in the afternoon. He took four. Could sense Kate observe him, forming some kind of opinion. He put a shaky hand on the dash, waited for the numbness to wrap itself around him like a blanket.

After he calmed down, she said, "Let's go see Andrew."

His son. He didn't know what to expect.

Kate got his chair, helped him out of the truck. Chris wondered how the fuck he was going to get his chair up the steps into the kitchen. Then he saw what was different. The steps were gone, replaced with a brand new ramp. She saw Chris notice.

"Your dad. When he heard, when he realized..." She didn't know how to put it. "He started right away. Finished just before..." So much of what she was saying couldn't be spoken.

The image of his father, old and creaky, laying cement, knocked him for a loop. His son, Andrew stood in the doorway. So much taller, not a boy, a little man.

Chris's inability to run to his son was physically painful. There was wet in his eyes, making Andrew blurry.

"Andrew, go see your father."

Chris rubbed his eyes to get a better look at the boy, his boy, who stepped toward his father, mouth open, eyes afraid. Then Andrew was washed away by tears. Chris tried to remember something his father might have said to him at that age, some bit of wisdom, something to take strength from. But his father was a man of few words, of small gestures.

When Andrew got within reach, all Chris could do was cry and pat his son's shoulder.

"We missed you, Dad. Welcome home."

Chris knew Kate told him to say this. They probably rehearsed it. He wished he could control himself. Finally, he got enough breath to say, "Thanks, son."

"Andrew, maybe your dad will let you push him in the house." She was by the truck, frowning. At him? At her own troubles? Chris had no idea.

Andrew pushed Chris up the new ramp, into the house.

SIX

THE MORNING OF THE FUNERAL, Donovan dresses in his uniform. A chest full of medals catches the light, the Purple Heart, the Bronze Star. He slips his prosthesis into a shoe as polished as the black hearse that would be carrying the body of Chris Rogers.

His men, Donovan will always think of them as his men, Crash, Nelson and Doc, are at the steps of St. Elizabeth's Church. Dressed in matching uniforms, the green berets would make them stand out in any crowd. They make an imposing trio, with their game faces on, hundred yard stares burning holes in anyone that looks their way. He looks closer. Doc is too thin, his face gaunt, his clothes loose. Nelson, gone gray, looks as mean as ever. Crash looks almost unchanged, like he just stepped out of the recruiter's office.

Donovan stands in front of them. He doesn't need to thank them. They nod and smile.

"Captain, you still using that cane to get sympathy from the ladies?" Crash takes a last puff of his cigarette.

"Soldier, I will use any and all means at my disposal to take down my opponent." The familiar phrase rolls off his tongue, too long since he's seen these boys, not boys anymore. He knew them when they were boys, before they'd killed a soul. He turned them into fighting machines, hard as diamonds.

The church bell reminds them where they are, time to go inside. They remove their berets. The church is cold and quiet. An organ hums, incense burns reminding the soldiers of cordite. The guest of honor arrives in a coffin. The congregation stands. Bagpipes. "Amazing Grace." The coffin on wheels pushed by the undertaker is followed by the pallbearers, then Chris's mother, then his widow and his son.

Kate wears a simple black dress. No veil. Donovan thinks about veils, wonders if the reason widows once wore them to funerals was to save others from having to witness their tears. Watching Kate's brave, sad, beautiful face, he wishes veils were still worn. It is difficult to endure her expression, but he can't turn away.

Something predatory in her eyes. She scans the church, searching, for someone to blame. A huntress, Donovan thinks.

It is a full mass, an Irish priest presides. Father Maher speaks with a light brogue, just right for sad occasions. "'Tis a terrible occasion which brings us together today," he says.

Donovan is well acquainted with terrible occasions. He hasn't been to church in a long time, not since he was a boy. Churches evoked deep thoughts and memories, something he tried to avoid. What if he'd remained in his hometown, he wonders. Took over his father's store. What would that have been like? Mass every Sunday. A son or daughter to take care of. He looks at the bowed head of Andrew Rogers.

The price of family is loss.

Donovan deals in death, in loss, but for him, life is cheap. Everyone's but his own. His is a life without intimacy. So why come here? Why put himself through this? Maybe he wants to see if he can still feel anything. Find out if he is still human. The emotions that stir in Donovan's chest are unfamiliar. He's not sure what they will make him do. They will not let him leave just yet.

He tries to remember the last time he spoke to his parents, his father. A month ago? Two? A vicious cycle, talking to them made him feel guilty, which made him put off calling, which made him feel guiltier. And the last time he actually saw them in person? Three years? Four? Too long.

Donovan comes back to the funeral. The priest is talking.

"There is always a temptation to play the *What if*

game. What if we'd done this? What if this hadn't happened?" The kind old eyes look out at the congregation as if forgiving them all for being human. "'Tis a dangerous game, this *What if*, and not very productive. Because in the end, ladies and gentlemen, there is no *What if*. There is only what happens. God has a plan for all his children. So you might ask yourselves, What if Chris Rogers hadn't died this way? You might as well ask, What if he had never been born? Where would we all be now?"

Donovan pictures his corpse, shredded by bullets at that rally in Kandahar, pictures his fellow soldiers laying lifeless next to him. They would all be in the ground if Chris Rogers had never been born. He looks at them, sees the knowledge in their eyes.

He has to find out who did this to Chris Rogers. Won't ask the others for help, but he knows they will. Kate Rogers puts an arm around her son. Who will put an arm around her? For Chris, he tells himself, convinces himself, we will do this for Chris.

On the way to the cemetery, in his rental car, Donovan doesn't listen to the radio. Alone with is thoughts he can't help noticing good spots for ambushes, dangerous intersections, suspicious cars. He'd forgotten the constricted maze of one-way streets and rotaries that makes up Greater Boston. Lots of places for snipers. Lots of blind alleys to hide in.

Walking through the graveyard, Donovan knows

where he would seek cover in case of enemy fire. By instinct he is aware of the high ground, of possible exit routes.

He joins the crowd huddled in a semi-circle around the coffin. Scans the horizon. His eyes zero in on a figure leaning against a tree in the distance. The silhouette is unmistakable, the man Kate threw out of the wake. Nathan. The priest hums his blessings. The Our Father is chanted. Holy water is sprinkled. Amen.

The undertaker says, "The family would like you to join them at Camille's after the service. Please ask for directions if you need them."

Donovan asks.

It takes time for the mourners to get to their cars and leave. Everybody knows everybody, small conversations break out and slow everything down. The soldiers congregate at Donovan's car.

"What's with the dude behind the tree?"

Donovan grins. Old habits die hard. "Name's Nate. The widow threw him out of the wake last night."

"No shit?"

"Is that our killer, Captain?"

"Maybe."

"But we're staying until we find him, right?"

"I'm staying." He doesn't take his eyes off Nate.

"Captain, if it's all the same–"

"Whoever wants to stay can stay."

They're all staying.

The cars begin to drive away.

"Okay. Let's leave with the crowd then double back. See what he's up to."

"We got company."

Kate and her boy. People whisper to her as she passes them, then slip into their cars. Andrew looks uncomfortable in his suit. A black suit, no doubt bought for the occasion. He holds his mother's hand. They stop in front of Donovan.

"I hope you're able to make it to the restaurant."

He smiles. "Wouldn't miss it. I believe I owe your son a story."

Andrew's eyes brighten at this news.

"That's right. I'm looking forward to it too." She turns to the others. "Thanks so much for coming, gentlemen."

Andrew clears his throat. "Did you all know my dad?" His expression makes them see the war as the boy must see it, a place where men go to lose their legs.

Crash says, "He saved us all, son. Your dad was a hero. Straight up."

Mother and son are incredulous. A hero? Chris Rogers? The thrill in Andrew's eyes is tempered by Kate's skepticism, but you can tell, she wants to believe it.

SEVEN

—

THE FUNERAL CROWD gets in their cars and leaves the cemetery in a centipede procession. The ghost of Chris Rogers watches, standing, yes, standing on top of his grave. Not a bad turnout, he thinks. Seeing his son was the most painful part. He was surprised to see the soldiers here.

The graves of his parents are just a few plots over. "Anybody here?" he whispers. No. He takes some comfort in that. He won't be trapped in this graveyard for eternity. But he would like to talk to them, see them. Only two senses have remained in death: sight and sound. How he misses the other three. The incense at the church he couldn't smell. Wind tickles the leaves of the trees making them shimmer, but Chris cannot feel the breeze. He reaches for his gravestone but his ghost hands pass right through it, like they passed through his wife and his son. He misses touch. Misses taste, even the feel of his tongue against his teeth would be nice.

Nate approaches the grave. Haggard, unshaven, wild bloodshot eyes, he looks haunted. He is haunted. He stands at the foot of the fresh dirt, jumpy, his head keeps turning, checking over his shoulder.

Chris notices the soldiers watching. Donovan and the other three are observing from a hill at the other end of the cemetery.

"You're dead, motherfucker." Nate glares at the tombstone. "I know. I shot you. I'm standing on your grave." He wipes tears out of his eyes. "You were a son of a bitch, too. Treated me like garbage ever since that day on the baseball field."

Chris does not want to hear this. Feels a surge where his heart used to be, a tightening in his phantom chest.

"Stole the only girl that looked twice at me." Nate sniffs. "Stop talking to me."

"Stop talking to me!" Chris's voice sends birds cawing into the air, crows, blue jays, swallows, a feathery explosion.

Nate crouches, arms up in surrender, eyes like two sunny side up eggs.

Chris leans close, whispering now, "They're coming for you, Nate."

Nate, his face the color of chalk, looks across the cemetery, at the soldiers. A whiter shade of pale now, shaking, Nate stands and stumbles away.

EIGHT

CAMILLE IS ONE OF THOSE authentic Italian restaurants that doesn't exist west of Chicago. Red and white checkered table cloths, waiters straight from the old country, a red sauce so good you clean your plate with the bread until it's clean enough to serve on again. Donovan hasn't eaten food like this in ages. On the walls, pictures of Sinatra, Dean Martin, Mario Lanza, their music belts out of the speakers.

The soldiers sit a little apart, at a corner table, the only thing out of the ordinary in this scene. Everybody else plays their usual part, like they have all their lives. Donovan observes what normal life would be like. A large room full of family and friends. A wife, a kid. He wonders who will be at his funeral. His parents, if they're still around. His brother. A few uncles and aunts might show up but he hasn't talked to any of his extended family in decades.

By the bar, some rowdy uncles are telling dirty jokes. The aunts are all fawning over a newborn nephew, one month old, sleeping on a table in the middle of the restaurant. The new mother beams. A pack of kids aged ten to thirteen tears through the place, screaming and giggling, thick as thieves. Andrew is among them, a sly smile on his face, Donovan is relieved to see.

Camille, the owner, a short, round little woman asks the soldiers how their food is.

Crash puts his fingers to his lips then kisses them open.

"Perfect, ma'am," Nelson says and they all agree.

Camille grins and scampers to the next table.

"So Captain," Doc says, serious now. "What do you make of the dude at the cemetery?"

Donovan washes a bite down with a sip of Chianti. "Same as you. He's either our trigger man or knows who is."

"So now what?" Crash says.

"We lean on him."

Andrew leads his gang of cousins and friends to Donovan's table. Their eyes, curious, skeptical, hungry for a story. Donovan tells them a watered down version. How Andrew's father noticed an Afghan sniper, hit him just as he was aiming at me. Donovan lifts his pant leg, shows the kids the titanium shaft of his lower leg, his metal foot. He hits it with his cane and they giggle at the noise.

The room is quiet now, everyone listening to the lies that spin out of his mouth.

"What were you doing there?" Andrew asks.

Donovan squints at him. "I could tell you, but then I'd have to kill you."

"A secret mission?" Andrew's eyes are delirious at the thought.

"That's why your father never talked about it."

The faces in the room go serious again, remember why they are here.

"I've probably told you too much as it is." Donovan notices Kate listening from a few tables over, her expression hard to read.

"What do you do now?" Andrew asks.

Reluctantly, Donovan breaks eye contact with Kate to look at Andrew. "I'm afraid that's classified too, Andrew."

The children are too excited to remain still, like a flock of small birds they dash from table to table, Andrew in the lead. The adults come alive with conversation, chattering now, no doubt, about Donovan's tale. Turning it in their heads, wondering, fairy tale or true story? He knows the story will evolve with each retelling through the neighborhood. He hopes Chris Rogers will only grow more heroic. Become some sort of folk hero.

Someone's aunt or grandmother tells the kids to go

play on the sidewalk. "Stay off the street," she hollers after them.

"Andrew, that means you," Kate says.

Donovan remembers his brother and himself as children. In the summer, from sun up to sun down they would roam the wilderness surrounding their house. With no supervision, like young bear cubs, they explored the world. They might wander all day and not see another human. Not like here. You can't escape people here. It was in his youth, he supposes, that he developed his love of solitude. Those moments, alone, with the wind in your ears, the sound of a creature dashing through the ferns, bird calls, babbling brooks.

He stands and walks outside. The children, mostly boys, have taken possession of the sidewalk, a pack of wolves, they prowl their territory.

Here traffic replaces the sound of water. The wind carries the different scents of the city, too many people doing too many things.

"How do you like Dot?" He hadn't noticed her standing right behind him. The racket of the city makes it easy to sneak.

"Dot?"

She chuckles. "It's what us locals call it. Dorchester."

He can pick her scent out of the air now. A flower. Lilacs? "It's crowded."

A quick, playful frown, then a smile. "It is.

Everybody right on top of each other. Everybody knows everybody's business."

"You grew up here?"

"Yeah. A block over."

The kids, shirts untucked now, hair askew, play tag. Andrew is it.

"Did you know Chris growing up?"

"Everybody knew Chris. He was a big athlete. Baseball. Football.

Donovan pictures Chris and Kate as kids. Walking to school. Kate young and skinny, hair in pig tails, smiling freckled face. A city girl. Now a widow, a single mother. Her sadness a stain that won't come out, just fade over time.

She rolls her eyes, senses his thoughts. "Don't go feelin' sorry for me, Captain."

He presses his lips into a thin smile. "Call me Patrick."

A toughness in her eyes now like when she yelled at Nate in the funeral home. "We'll be okay, Patrick."

"Who was the guy at the funeral home?"

"What guy?"

"You know what guy."

Her eyes go flat. "Nate Riley."

"Did he do it?"

"Ask the cops."

"I'm asking you."

"I don't know." Her hands are balled into fists. "I wouldn't put it past him."

Andrew has a child over his shoulder.

"Andrew, put Brian down."

The boy follows his mother's instructions.

Kate lets out a sigh. "Nate Riley. You know, he wasn't a bad kid back in the day. Got picked on. 'Cause of the way he looked." She chew her lip. "It turned him mean."

"Did Chris pick on him?"

"Yeah, he did."

"Doesn't make it right. If Nate did it."

"No, it doesn't."

Donovan has to look away as tears gather in the corners of her eyes. Doesn't trust himself not to try to rub them away, not to take her in his arms, pull her slender figure tight against his chest.

Down the road, three men walk with purpose toward him. Two tall, broad men behind, one short and wide in front. Nate Riley and two goons.

"Looks like we've got some visitors," Donovan says.

"Christ," Kate says.

The men close in, all three wear cheap sunglasses. The tall ones are in t-shirts and long leather coats. Nate's suit fits him badly, a toothpick pokes out of his mouth.

The kids stop their game, turn into rabbits watching a predator.

Donovan tightens and relaxes his arms and legs, discreetly, opens and closes his hands, takes a few deep breaths through his nose.

Nate stops in front of Kate. "Nice to see you, Kate," he says out of the sneer on his face.

Her answer is a shivery silence.

Nate's sneer turns grimace. "Well, I think we both know you're a little behind on your payments."

Donovan rolls his head back and forth, loosens his neck.

Nate removes his sunglasses. "Hey, I'm a sensitive guy. I know you've had some troubles. I can extend protection for a week. After that, well, let's not test it. Like Chris did."

A tremor passes through Kate's bulging eyes.

"Give my best to your parents." The cheap mirror shades go back on. Nate turns to walk away.

"You don't need to wait a week." Donovan summons his old military bark. "She's not paying you now and she's not paying you then."

Nate keeps walking.

"You hard of hearing, shorty?"

That stops him. The three men turn around.

"Who the hell are you?"

"Just the guy telling you how it is."

Nate shakes his head, grins. "There must be some confusion. Because that's my name. Because that's my job. But you sound like you're from out of town.

Maybe you're a little confused. Charlie, go give Mr. the guy telling me how it is a nice Dorchester welcome."

One of the hulks smiles and marches at Donovan.

Patrick's teeth are showing too. His body buzzes, his stomach tingles. It's been a while since he squared off with someone and he's missed it. He doesn't really need the cane to walk. His prosthesis keeps him nicely balanced. The cane is mostly a deception, but it serves another purpose.

He waits until the tall man is almost upon him before gripping the cane two-handed, like a samurai sword, then spins, the titanium shaft whistles through the air, the tip lands flush on the man's nose, sits him down in an explosion of blood, his nose surely broken.

The kids on the sidewalk gasp.

Nate's fat jaw flexes. He narrows his eyes at Donovan and sighs. "Charlie, get the fuck up."

Like a drunken sailor, Charlie pulls himself up on wobbly legs.

Nate looks at Kate. "One week." To Donovan, "Watch your back, soldier."

Donovan winks and blows him a kiss.

A furious chuckle escapes Nate's lips.

When the three men have walked out of sight, the children begin to reenact Donovan's exploits with Charlie.

Kate looks confused. "Did that just happen?"

The familiar taste of adrenaline, the quickening of

his heart, is a welcome sensation. But there is something new now, here, something he hasn't felt in so long he'd forgotten how much he missed it. Righteous. Too long since he fought the good fight. He forgot how much of a difference it makes. A swelling of his heart rather than a shrinking. Pride instead of shame.

Although the way Kate looks at him and the awe on the faces of Andrew and his cousins. This is pleasant too.

His men are in the doorway. He knew they were ready to get involved if needed. They can sense how he feels. They are jealous. They want to feel like that too. Like the good guy, the man wearing a white hat, riding a white horse. Just once more. He can see it in their faces.

Kate's eyes are closed. "This is going to be trouble."

"Probably," Donovan says.

"Nate can't just let this go." She brushes a stray hair back behind her ear. "What the hell are you smiling at?"

"Sorry. We need to be ready. Nate'll come back, maybe tonight, maybe tomorrow, maybe a week."

"What are you talking about?"

"Oh. Me and the boys. We'll stick around."

His men are next to him.

"What's the plan?" Nelson says.

Donovan's voice is calm and commanding. "We'll

need a four man kit. Small firearms. Nothing too fancy. Nothing mounted."

"Copy that." Nelson pulls out his phone, dials.

Donovan: "Crash, take the car, get to know the perimeter. Lots of one-way streets here."

"Roger."

"Doc, get back to the store. Babysit."

Doc starts to walk away but Donovan catches him, pulls him close.

"You up for this, Doc? You need to get back?"

"Get your fucking hands off me, Captain."

Donovan loosens his grip. "Pardon me."

"Meet you back at the ranch."

The ranch is how they will refer to the store and the apartment now. This will be their base, the place they need to secure and protect.

"What is happening?" Kate says.

"We're gonna get these people off your back."

She chuckles without an ounce of humor. "You don't know the people you're talking about. That's just how it is in this neighborhood, the way it's always been. You think you can change that?"

"We're gonna give it a try."

"Chris tried."

Back inside the restaurant the only topic is the encounter between Donovan and Nate. The younger half of the room is thrilled, the older half nervous. Kate lands right in the middle, half excited, half terrified.

After, Donovan walks Kate and Andrew back to the ranch. He clocks every movement with his hawk eyes, every car that passes, knows the position of every pedestrian, on the lookout for any ambush spot. He is back in the zone, back in Kandahar, in Fallujah. Super aware, ready for anything.

They pass bar after bar on Dorchester Avenue, Donovan can almost hear the news travel, rumors of what happened between him and Nate's thugs. He meets the eyes of the neighborhood toughs observing him from windows and doorways. Strange to feel it here, the knowledge of being a foreign threat. These men, and some women, look at him like the Taliban did, like they wanted him drawn and quartered.

Kate whispers, "Well, you've certainly made a name for yourself."

It isn't all hard looks. From the Korean laundromat, curious, frightened eyes. Likewise the kosher bakery. Dorchester isn't as homogeneous as it once was. All the more reason for the old guard to flex their muscles.

Kate talks, maybe because she's nervous, maybe because she likes to talk, about how this news will travel. Like a virus through the bloodstream, first the bars will get it, the waiters and waitresses from Camille's stopping for a shot and a beer will bend the ears of the barflies and bartenders, the pool hustlers, the bookies, the drug dealers, the cops, the firemen, the dockworkers. Andrew's young cousins will tell their friends, in a day or two all the kids in Dot will know the story.

Sooner than later the story will get to Daddy McMahon.

"Who's Daddy McMahon?"

She smiled like a parent at an ignorant child. "He runs things in our neck of the woods."

"Why do they call him Daddy?"

"He looks like Daddy Warbucks. From Annie."

"So nothing happens in this neighborhood without his say so?"

"Nope."

"Did you kill a lot of people in Afghanistan?"

"Andrew."

He has not left Donovan's side the entire walk. Head high, chest puffed, he is full of pride at the company he keeps.

Donovan ponders the question. "What's a lot?"

Andrew squints an eye, chews a lip, in thought. "Ten."

Donovan nods. "Yes, I killed a lot of people in Afghanistan." He's killed a lot of people since Afghanistan.

The boy's eyes bulge, his jaw drops. "Whoa." He bounces next to Donovan as he walks. "Was it more than ten? How many?"

"Enough, Andrew."

NINE

—

DONOVAN HAS NO IDEA how many people he's killed, or whose deaths he is responsible for. Only serial killers keep track of these things. Or flying aces. Or assassins. He considers himself a failed assassin. He likes to think most of them had it coming, but the ghosts of the young girl who perished in Chris Rogers' arms and Wali Karzai's bodyguard tell him different. But he was just an instrument of the government back then, just following orders. Right? What about now? He associates almost exclusively with drug dealers, thieves, gangsters, as though protecting the general public from himself.

He looks at the boy and Kate and wonders what danger he is exposing them to. Everything he touches seems to die.

The judge had told him, "Whether you intend to be or not, Mr. Donovan, you are a menace to society.

Your records clearly indicate that you seek conflict out. The court appreciates your service to this country, your sacrifice. The rules of combat do not apply within our borders, soldier."

He almost laughed, knew it wasn't in his best interest. The rules of combat. As if there were any.

"I see you're willing to seek counseling, attend therapy sessions?"

"Yes, your honor." His lawyer's idea.

"Do us all a favor, Mr. Donovan. Listen to what they have to say. With both ears."

"Yes, your honor."

"Six months of therapy. To be started within one month. Dismissed."

"Thank you, your honor," his lawyer told him to say.

He alternated, group therapy one week, one on one sessions with a counselor the next. At the VFW Hospital. Donovan was both relieved and depressed to discover he was far from the most fucked up person in the room. His was not the only missing limb. Hank had only his right arm, grotesquely muscled, but he was grateful for that one limb. They all suffered from nightmares, saw dead people in their sleep.

Their group leader, Steve, wore a black patch over his right eye. He lifted it, showed the hollow socket where his eye used to be, a lightning bolt scar where the shrapnel sliced his eye in half. He shrugged, "We've all got our scars to bear."

"I'm the eight dwarf," Hank liked to joke. "Stumpy."

They shared their bitter stories, drank bitter coffee.

Donovan outranked them all, mostly enlisted, all men. Didn't take him long to realize he was the only real killer among them. He did not say much the first session.

The next week he met with Steve in his office, a dingy room that must have been a janitor's closet at one point, Donovan could smell wet mops and Mr. Clean. Colorful self-help book spines mixed with fat volumes of history, Donovan saw Gibbon. There was barely room for the second chair next to Steve's desk, where Donovan was invited to sit.

"Shut the door, man. Let's have some privacy." Steve's voice was gentle, the kind of forced gentle you use when talking to the mentally ill or toddlers, or the elderly, like you were terribly sorry to have to tell them the way it is.

Donovan shut the door, set his cane against the wall, folded his hands in his lap.

Difficult to read Steve's expression with the eye patch on, everything turned slightly sinister. "So how's it going, Captain?"

"Fine."

"Fine, huh?" Steve had a folder open in front of him. "That's how you'd describe things?"

"Today, yes. Things are fine."

Steve pursed his lips, nodded. "Would you say

things were fine two months ago at the American Spirit?"

That was the bar where Donovan had hospitalized two men, seriously injured four others. "No, I would not."

"But now things are fine?"

"Today things are fine."

"What about tomorrow?"

"I try not to think too far ahead."

"What about yesterday?"

"I try not to dwell on the past."

"Really?"

"Really."

"How'd you lose that foot?"

"I don't remember."

Steve chuckled. "Nice. Okay, tough guy. You're lookin' to just coast, do your time, get the courts off your back, I can respect that. But something's eating at you, whether you want to admit it or not. You just gonna let it swallow you up?"

"Maybe."

"Suit yourself. Ever think maybe you need an outlet for that dark side of yours?"

"What dark side?"

Steve bit his lower lip, seemed to consider something, then decided to say, "Special forces, huh? Ranger?"

"Hooah."

"You know where the ladies' room is in the west side of the JFK Building at Fort Benning?"

This got Donovan's attention. It was an inside joke. There was no ladies' room. Built in the sixties, they did not anticipate the need for one. As it happened, there still wasn't much of a need. "Do you?"

Steve smiled. "Ain't one. Now what was I saying?"

"An outlet for my dark side. Like going to Karate lessons, taking up running?"

"I might know a guy."

"A guy?"

"Another guy who knows the answer to the question I just asked you. Maybe he could use a guy like you."

"A guy like me?"

"A tough guy with a dark side."

"What are you, some kind of recruiter? Is there a finder' fee?"

"Something like that." Steve sighed, one of those dog tired, world weary sighs that Donovan knew so well. "Look, I'm here to help people. Veterans. You want to get better, fine, let's talk about your drinking, let's talk about the pills you're popping." He stared at Donovan with his ornery good eye.

He thought of John Wayne in True Grit. Steve had true grit.

"I've been doing this a while. Since Iraq one. I know

a lost cause when I see one. Your war wasn't like theirs. I think you know that."

"How's this work?"

"I set up a meet."

"Where?"

A round trip ticket to Vegas. A reservation in a suite at the Four Seasons in Mandalay Bay. Once the plane passed Colorado, the western deserts and mountains soothed him, their shape and color a familiar song. Vegas arched up all of a sudden, a neon volcano erupting out of the desert. Even in the airport, the white noise of fluorescent lighting and air conditioning was drowned out by the cheap dinging of slot machines, the clownish pulse of the circus city. It made for a dizzy feeling. A man in a black suit held a sign that read, 'Donovan.' He introduced himself. A large Mexican, the man only nodded and directed him to where the limo was parked. Donovan only had a carry on, no other baggage to claim. He was returning in two days according to his ticket.

"*Como te llámas*?" Donovan asked.

"Juan."

Juan put Donovan's bag in the trunk, opened the back door. Donovan slid into the lush leather seats. The divider was up. He found a news station on the radio. A suicide bomb in Kabul, an IED took out a Humvee. Twenty Americans would be coming home in boxes. He tapped his fake foot with his cane, wondered about the injured.

The city, all glass and light, sparkled under the sledgehammer Nevada sun but Donovan's eyes were drawn to the horizons, the surrounding mountains and sand. Plenty of space to bury a body or two.

The walls of the Mandalay Bay Hotel were made of gold, fool's gold no doubt, and the late sun mirrored off the west side of the building and blinded anyone in its sight.

Juan guided him past the normal check-in line to a separate desk for the Four Seasons. Once Donovan was greeted, Juan disappeared. The woman at the desk welcomed him to Las Vegas. He was all set, no credit card required. Did he need anything? No, m' am. The elevator glided up to the top floors. His room had a view of the whole world. He sat and enjoyed it. He was sure there was a full bar, but for some reason, he didn't crave a thing.

Later the phone rang.

"How's the room working out, partner?" A Texas twang.

"Fine."

"Well that's fine. Was hoping we could get that meeting out of the way."

"When."

"Right now."

"Sounds good."

"Be right there."

The Texan was thin and blonde, dressed in a light gray suit, black cowboy boots and a black cowboy hat which he removed when he stepped into the room. They shook hands. "You can call me Walker, Captain."

"Okay, Walker."

The Texan smiled. "Mind if I get a drink?"

"It's your party, Walker."

Walker nodded, went to the bar, dropped his hat on the counter. "Can I get you something?"

"What are you having?"

"I'm a bourbon man. On the rocks. When I'm in fucking Vegas, it's gotta be on the rocks."

"Make it two."

"Good man." Walker poured two glasses, handed one to Donovan.

They sat in the living room. Sipped their drinks. Walker had a pistol in a shoulder holster under his suit.

He tapped it. "If this bothers you, I could take it off."

"It's no problem."

"Force of habit."

"So how does this work?"

"Different ways. Depends on you. But we start small."

"How small?"

"A security job. Hector Escondido and his wife and daughter are coming to town. He's got a meeting.

The ladies want to see a show. You know Hector Escondido?"

"No."

"Drug kingpin, with a Mexican Cartel. Not a bad guy, as ruthless gangsters go. The jobs I'm offering, he's about as sweet as they come."

"Doesn't he have his own men?"

Walker nodded. "In Mexico, he travels with a small army. Not so easy to do in the states. When he's in town, he lets me know what he needs."

"What show are they seeing?"

"Cirque du Soleil. *O*. At the Bellagio ."

"When?"

"Tomorrow night. Here's a ticket for tonight. Scout the location, see the show. Get the lay of the land."

Donovan took the ticket.

"Here's some walking around money. I assume you need a piece?"

"Yup."

"What do you like?"

"Maybe a Beretta?"

"Okay, James Bond. It'll show up here tonight with a shoulder rig. Tomorrow, I'll let you know when and where." Walker handed Donovan a cell phone. "Keep that on you. I'm in your contact list if something comes up."

The Beretta showed up in a small case, delivered by a bellhop, unlocked. The holster was in a separate zipped bag that also contained ammo. Donovan chuckled as he put the leather straps on over his shirt, wondered if the boy had peaked at what he was delivering. He inspected the pistol. He had to admit, he'd missed the feel of a weapon. Its weight in his hand or under his coat, reassuring and dangerous.

Outside the window, Vegas lights shot holes in the night. He had a nice view of the Lagoon show at the Treasure Island Casino, a battle between two ships.

So this is what I've become, he thought, a pirate, a mercenary. Beat picking fights in dive bars, waking up in the drunk tank. He hadn't even finished the drink Walker poured him. When was the last time that had happened? Instinct told him to take it easy, stay sharp.

He went to the show. Plenty of exits, easy to get out in a hurry. Lots of places to hide. He looked up at the light rigging in the ceiling. Plenty of places. The show itself was strange, like being trapped in the mind of some European child on acid. He paid attention to everything, wanted to notice any differences tomorrow night.

The familiar electricity, he was a man with a mission. It felt good. In his room, he stripped down to his underwear and worked out. His muscles squawked but he knew tomorrow the burn would feel good. After a week, his muscles would fall in line.

He dreamed of the desert. Stood at the end of a shallow grave. Another man at the head of the hole in the ground. Was it Donovan's grave? He knew this dream, the only constants the desert and a grave. The man changed, sometimes younger, sometimes older, sometimes it was his father. It wasn't always a man. Might be a woman or a girl. Sooner or later, Donovan would be in the grave. The ending was always the same. The young girl from Afghanistan looked down at him. He just noticed the tears in her eyes, when he woke up.

He'd been up for hours when the phone rang. It was Walker.

"Meet the driver in the lobby. He'll take you to the airport. Lands in an hour."

He dressed in his gangster clothes. Donovan new the importance of uniforms. It helped supply expectations. Important to look the part. Black suit, black shoes, white shirt, a close shave, a mean look.

The driver's name was Reggie. He wore the same uniform, but added a pair of mirror sunglasses. His kinky hair was in a short fro, the only thing that kept him from looking like a secret service man. Reggie's hand, when Donovan shook it, was a bear paw. His eyes, like everybody's, went right to the cane.

"So you're the new guy?" His voice a low growl, if a grizzly could talk.

"How long you been on this beat?"

"Five years, give or take."

"And?"

"I'm just labor, man. I drive. Point A to point B."

"Okay. You know the Escondidos?

"Yup."

"Anything you can tell me, or are you just a driver?"

A toothless smile. "Mrs. Escondido's high maintenance, trophy wife, cokehead. The kid's just a kid."

"Thanks. Let's go get them."

Donovan and Reggie met the Escondidos at baggage claim. They recognized Reggie who proceeded to take their bulging luggage off the turnstile.

"Senor Escondido, Patrick Donovan, at your service."

"Buenos tardes, Señor."

Escondido introduced his wife and his daughter, Rosa. Mrs. Escondido dressed like a latin porn star, tight, low top, short skirt. Makeup like war paint on her face. She looked beautiful and mean. She squinted at Donovan like she was looking at a garbage man. Who was he to argue?

Donovan sat in the front with Reggie.

"How were my descriptions?"

"Spot on, Reggie."

Rosa had her mother's beautiful face and her father's tendency towards chubbiness. She stayed close to her father and leaned away from her mother.

Reggie drove to the Bellagio, an Italian fortress in the center of the strip, opulent and shining, water fountains rose ten stories into the sky made the air itself dazzle.

Donovan's eyes clocked the lobby, taking inventory in an instant. He was the only man, besides Escondido, packing heat. Twenty three guest in the room, four behind the desk, six bell hops, fourteen men, six women, three children. He added and subtracted as people came and went. Check in took seconds. A man brought the Escondidos luggage in on a rolling rack.

At the suite, Donovan asked the Escondidos to wait while he checked things out. Marble floors in the halls, thick carpeting in the rooms, decadent furniture. The views made this room seem like the top of the world. All clear. Escondido nodded and walked in, followed by Mrs. Escondido and Rosa. Their daughter could not take her eyes off Donovan's cane. Her mother headed straight to the mini bar, poured herself a vodka on the rocks. She took the drink into the master bedroom. Rosa sat on a couch, pulled out her smartphone and checked her texts.

Escondido sat next to his daughter, sighed. "You were a soldier, Señor Donovan?"

"Yes."

"Where?"

"Iraq. Afghanistan. A few other places."

Escondido pointed to the cane. "This happened over there?"

"Afghanistan. Yes."

Escondido nodded. "And still you live the warrior's life?"

"You could say that."

"I will." The gangster's eyes were playful. "I will say that. I wonder, did you try to give it up? Walk the straight and narrow path."

Donovan smiled a thin smile. "You could say that."

Escondido chuckled. "For some men violence is like a religion. Without it, they are lost. Are you one of these men, Señor Donovan?"

"I guess I am."

"Bueno. Let's drink to it. What will you have?"

Escondido stood, walked to the bar, poured a tequila, raised his eyebrows at Donovan.

"Bourbon. Neat."

"*Muy bien.*"

He sipped his Maker's Mark, savored the angry burn of it on his tongue, in his gut.

Escondido made his way to the master bedroom.

Donovan looked out at the Strip as its neon lights seemed to siphon light out of the sky. The western horizon glowed red like a wound. Two men would be coming soon to escort Escondido to the big Cartel meeting. He looked at his watch. Any minute now.

"Mr. Donovan, you are here to protect us?" Rosa's English was good. Just a slight accent. English learned watching MTV in between lessons.

"Yes, Rosa."

"From who?"

Donovan looked toward the master bedroom. "Bad men."

Rosa did not look at Donovan, just continued to type on her smartphone. "Ah. Bad men. Like my father?"

"You think your father is a bad man?"

"Mr. Donovan, I know he is." She looked up at him now.

A knock on the door broke the silence, allowed Donovan to turn away from the eyes of this child who was smarter than her years. He went to the door.

"Yeah?" He looked out at the two men in dark suits.

"Harry sent us." The phrase they had arranged as a password.

Donovan opened the door.

Big men, linebackers. Six foot three or four, wide as barn doors, arms like tree limbs. Too big for Special Forces who preferred lean men who could blend into crowds, disappear when needed. These two were all about being noticed, using their size to intimidate.

Rosa made a startled noise in her throat when she saw them.

Something strange, Donovan thought. Their coats were open and the second man seemed about to reach for his piece but stopped.

"Where's Escondido?" the first man asked, voice smooth. Maybe it was nothing.

"In the bedroom. I'll let him know you're here."

Donovan walked to the bedroom, exaggerating his need for the cane.

"Señor Escondido, your escort is here."

"Excellent, just a minute."

When Donovan came back into the main room, he saw the same movement from the second man. An itchy trigger finger.

Old soldiers know the moment. The moment of kill or be killed. They learn to recognize it – or they don't get old. Donovan recognized that the moment was almost here.

Couldn't just blow them away, though. Needed to catch them in the act. Rosa, oblivious, texted a friend. Was she on their list? And her mother? Or was it just Escondido?

Donovan went to that place he went, when the shit was about to go down and you were about to be standing in it up to you knees. When people were about to get smoked and maybe you were one of them. For those about to die, we salute you, Donovan thought. He flexed his hands, wiggled his fingers. Looked at the second man, whose eyes glowered, a bead of sweat like a tear ran down his head, more beads formed on top of his bald scalp. Donovan felt cool, he smiled at the second man.

Escondido's steps in the hallway, the tap of expensive leather shoes on marble floors. "*Hola hombres,*" he said as he walked into the living room.

Escondido did not see the first man pull his pistol out of his jacket and aim it at him. Rosa did. But by the time the scream escaped her mouth, Donovan had fired a round into the first man's head.

The second man, gun in hand, hesitated just a second, half a second, just long enough for Donovan to shoot him in the right shoulder. The man's gun clattered to the floor.

Rosa still screamed.

Swinging his cane like a baseball bat, Donovan took the second man's legs out from under him. Then his knee was on the man's throat. Then the butt of his Beretta slammed into the man's sweaty forehead. Now the barrel was aimed at his face. Donovan waited for the man's eyes to come back into focus.

"Hurts, don't it? Answer my questions or it's gonna hurt a lot more."

The man gritted his teeth.

"Rosa, go see your mother."

She was frozen, eyes unblinking.

"Rosa, *vaya*." Her father gently nudged her.

She ran to the bedroom.

Donovan turned back to the man underneath him, looked him in the eyes. Close to broken. "You working for Harry?"

When the man didn't answer, Donovan hit him in the nose. A satisfying splash of blood.

"Señor Escondido, pack up your family. We need to leave as soon as possible."

Escondido's eyes were furious but he nodded. It made sense.

Donovan nudged the man with his pistol, "You working for Harry?"

"Yes."

A good plan. Avoid the crowds in the casino or at the show. Keep it contained in a guest room. No cameras.

The Escondidos emerged from the bedroom just as Donovan kicked the man in the temple. Rosa's eyes were puffy. Mrs. Escondido looked highly irritated at having to carry her own bag.

"Please wait outside for a moment." Donovan met eyes with Escondido. It was understood what would happen once they were out the door. When it was done, Donovan took the phone out of the first man's pocket, it was identical to the one Harry had given Donovan, on which he now called Reggie, the driver.

"Hello?" Nervous.

"Reggie, did you know what was going down?"

A long pause. A deep breath followed by a sigh. "Look, I'm not management. I don't get details. But there was some writing on the wall."

"I need a ride to Mexico. Should I call someone else?"

Another pause. "I'll get you there. Lobby of Caesar's. Fifteen minutes."

"We're at the Bellagio."

"Everyone in town knows where you are. Get to Caesar's. Quick and quiet."

Dial tone.

The Escondidos were in the hallway. Mrs. Escondido cursed in Spanish. As the door close behind Donovan, she spit on the ground. Rosa looked shell shocked. Donovan had seen the expression on rookie soldiers their first day in combat, the first time someone tried to kill them, when the meaning of war finally sank into their thick, young heads.

"It's done?" Escondido said.

"It's done."

"We are betrayed?"

"Looks that way."

Mrs. Escondido in full bitch mode, "What now geniuses?"

"We leave town. Now. A car will meet us at the lobby of Caesar's."

"He can be trusted?" Escondido.

"We'll see."

Donovan did not like the look in Rosa's eyes, like she was looking at a replay of Donovan killing the first man over and over again, he didn't like how she shivered.

"Rosa? Rosa."

She blinked, looked at him.

"*Esta bien.* It'll be okay. *Vámonos.*"

Donovan walked. The family followed.

They made it to Caesar's without incident. Donovan could see the fury in Escondido's eyes, his trembling fists. No doubt he was picturing gruesome retribution.

Once in the lobby, Donovan pressed Harry's number on the first man's cell phone. It barely rang.

"Christ, Murphy." Harry's voice. "What was the hold up?"

"You know how it is, Harry," Donovan kept his voice flat and calm, almost amused. "You've got to be ready for complications."

"Donovan?"

"Harry, find a nice comfortable hiding place. Don't worry about trying to find me. I'll find you soon enough."

He threw both phones away.

Reggie was right on time. In a yellow cab now.

"What's this?"

"My getaway car. Clean plates, registration. We'll switch cars again to go across the border."

Mrs. Escondido was less than impressed. No one else really cared what she thought. Donovan in the front. Escondidos in the back. Rosa was asleep before they left the city limits. Reggie drove west. Other than the smooth roads, it felt to Donovan like he was back in Afghanistan in the dark limbo of the desert. He held his pistol tight, braced for roadside bombs.

He felt good. Not tired. He had sleepwalked through the last few years. Now he was awake. Death and killing will do that to a man, especially a soldier.

Escondido made calls. He cursed in Spanish and English, depending on who he talked to. He asked Donovan for advice.

Thus did Patrick Donovan become the chief lieutenant of the Escondido Cartel. He had gotten a taste of battle. Hadn't realized how bad he'd craved it.

"*Amigo*," Escondido said, "There is only one way to run this business. Ruthless."

Within a month, Donovan had killed more men than in ten years of military service.

He remembered the first one. Not a Mexican, a DEA agent. Donovan was told he was dirty, maybe he was, it didn't matter. He was in the wrong place at the wrong time. Donovan needed a scalp to keep the wolves at bay, Escondido's foot soldiers, eyeing him like lions eye their tamer, waiting for a moment's weakness to pounce. Donovan made it quick, shot him in the face, so he wouldn't have to look at his dead eyes, so he couldn't see himself in the dead cop's face.

Instead, he saw his old friend, King. Shot the same way, maybe for the same reason. King's ghost whispered in his ear, *What have you become?*

They needed to dispose of the body.

A ride out to the desert, Donovan and five of Escondido's men, the DEA agent's corpse, and his ghost.

Escondido warned him, out in the Sonoran Desert there were no rules. His men might take matters into their own hands. Donovan was a threat. "Watch your back, amigo."

He observed the men, on the lookout for signs of betrayal. They avoided looking at him, their eyes shifty, hands touching their guns repeatedly. Donovan wouldn't touch his until he was going to use it.

"The hell are you doing down here in this forlorn place, with these godless men?" The ghost of the agent spoke in a deep whisper.

"It didn't used to be like this." King's ghost now. "We used to have a reason. We used to be the good guys."

We were never the good guys, Donovan thought. *We just thought we were. We're kidding ourselves. I was a killer then, I'm a killer now, but with no romantic illusions.*

In an old Chevy pickup, they drove past mountains, through valleys, far from any paved roads. Not hard for Donovan to imagine he was back in the Middle East. He sat in the back, with three other live men, one dead one. In the middle of an ocean of sand, the truck stopped. A graveyard with no headstones, he knew there were bodies planted six feet under for miles.

Donovan noticed the men look at each other. Knew,

the way he always knew, that it was now or never. Quick or dead...

Now. Quick.

The switchblade up his sleeve, now in his palm, click, a backhand stab into Sal's sternum. With his forehand stroke, Manny's throat became a bloody smile of a gash. Pablo's eyes bulged, his hand shook reaching for his pistol. Donovan ended him with a vampire slaying overhand thrust to the heart.

The man in the passenger seat stepped out of the cab, turned, saw the carnage. His cigarette fell out of his mouth. His skull exploded before the butt hit the ground.

The driver stood next to the truck frozen in place, pants piss stained, arms up in surrender. "*Por favor.*"

Donovan threw a shovel at him. "Start digging."

One big hole for Escondido's men. Donovan dug a separate hole for the slain agent. A pathetic gesture, but there it was.

The driver's name was Jesus. Just a kid, maybe sixteen or seventeen. A perfect witness to tell the tale of how Donovan had gone out to the desert with five of Escondido's men and come back with one. He knew the story might grow with every retelling, would discourage the rest of Escondido's soldiers from getting ideas.

On the way back, he tried to rationalize, made up excuses for the bodies he just buried. They had it coming. If he hadn't done it, he'd be buried back there. In the distance, on the side of the road, a small silhouette. As they drove closer it became a familiar young girl, her front stained a rusty red, clothes torn, dark eyes that saw through the lies he told himself. Knew he'd enjoyed the rush of it. Took pride in his prowess.

"Did you see that?" Donovan said.

The boy driving looked around at the desolate landscape. "See what?"

"Nada. Not a fucking thing."

After that, things got blurry. And bloody. And bloodier.

Juarez. A vampire city that came alive at night to feast on blood. Reached from America by bridges that should be etched with Dante's famous warning, *Abandon hope, all ye who enter here*. The surest way to die in that infernal city was to hope for better days. The front line of the cartel wars, danger around every corner, down every alley.

Most drop offs and pick ups occurred in the poorer sections of Juarez, in bars too dirty for rats, where the police did not venture at night.

Donovan had been around the globe. He knew the third world. He'd been to worse places, seen worse conditions, but not much worse. In places like this it was easy to see life as a cheap thing, which is why people seemed to risk it so casually. Dodging bullets for a pile of drugs or money, the girls risking disease or worse in the brothels for the same.

He got to know the brothels of Calle Mariscal and Avenida Juarez. They were easy places to hole up for a night, with no questions asked, no paper trail, and it allowed the men to blow off some steam, get drunk, get laid.

His taste in prostitutes became well known. Young, the youngest they had. Dark hair, dark skin. Little lost girls. Runaways. He would pay for the whole night. Sad-eyed girls with blank faces led him to their awful, tiny rooms. They would start to undress and he would stop them. Confusion on their faces. What now, their faces asked. What new horror to be inflicted upon them.

He just wanted to sleep. Told them to wake him if anyone came, if anything happened. These were the only nights he slept well, deep and dreamless, as though the child whores had the power to chase his demons away.

Rare that he was able to visit the same girl twice. Young women were the most disposable resource Juarez possessed. He gave them enough money to run away with. He tried to picture them somewhere safe, a humble village, a quaint house. But he knew better. Much easier to imagine them as victims of the terrible tastes of evil men.

As his own victims piled up, the legend of Long

John Silver grew, the gringo pirate from El Norte, with the peg leg. Even his own men feared him. When he walked into a bar, people's voices lowered, crowds parted.

Donovan couldn't deny, a part of him enjoyed it. He was reborn a villain.

Dark times.

Here, among the thugs and brigands of Mexico, things were much simpler than overseas. No political double dealing. Drugs, money, greed. Buyers and sellers. This was true transparency. If you saw an angle, you played it. If you could steal something, you took it. If you got caught, you died. No hard feelings. So simple.

He became numb to it. Justified his actions by arguing to himself, these were evil men. They were all on their way to hell, he just got them there faster.

So Donovan is surprised now by how bad he wants to save someone. Surprised and scared to find his soul still there, tattered and torn. Can *it* be saved?

TEN

A STRANGE PATH, his life, Donovan thinks. A path that has led here. Dorchester, Massachusetts. The Dot. To this neighborhood shop. In the dusky light it's hard to see until their feet are standing in the broken shards that the front windows have been shattered. Jagged glass borders the frames like shark teeth. They hear footsteps crunch from inside. Donovan's skin tingles. He is intensely aware that he is not carrying a weapon. Doc's head appears in the lion's mouth of a window.

He shrugs. "Just a couple cement blocks. I heard them burn rubber when I got here.

"Any damage inside?" Donovan says.

"Nope. All clear."

Kate sighs, relieved. She hugs her son.

Andrew surveys the damage with narrowed eyes. Easy, kid, Donovan thinks. Remembers the young kids in the service from Southie, from the Bronx, from

Compton. Remembers their anger at the world, at the injustices they saw. These kids always overreacted, wore their furious hearts on their sleeves. Donovan puts a hand on the boy's shoulder.

"Calm down, Andrew." He leaves his hand there until Andrew unclenches his fists.

"Let me get a few brooms," Kate says.

When she is in the back room, a Boston Police cruiser pulls up. Two uniforms step out. The passenger older, heavier, grayer, a salt and pepper moustache under a nose broken more than once. The driver is young, a blonde crew cut, his uniform tight on his biceps. Donovan realizes he and Doc are still in their uniforms from the funeral.

"Soldiers," the older cop says.

"Officers," Donovan says.

Now both sides know who is in charge.

The older one notices the boy. "Hey there, Andy. Your mom around."

"Hey, Mr. Emerson. Yeah, she's getting a broom."

Emerson nods. "You fellas here for the funeral?"

They nod.

"Goddamned shame," he says.

"Any of you see anything?" the younger cop asks.

Donovan and Doc both say, no.

"We were just getting back from the reception."

"Check with the neighbors, Johnny."

Johnny rolls his eyes. "You know what they'll say."

"Still gotta ask, kid."

Johnny walks next door.

Emerson turns to Donovan. "Did I hear there was a little excitement down there?"

Donovan does his best wide-eyed innocent look. "Nothing comes to mind, officer."

Emerson doesn't look surprised by the answer. "Where'd you serve, soldier?"

"All over. Mostly in the sand. You?"

"The jungle."

He has that way about him. The look of a man who learned everything he needed to know carrying an M-16 over his head as he waded through rice paddies.

"Bobby Emerson," Kate says, "someone call about a cat up a tree?"

"Ma'am that's the fire department."

Their smiles are genuine. They go back a ways.

"Well, I guess if someone had to come, I'm glad it's you, Bill."

"Girl, I'm getting awful tired of seeing you in black."

"You and me both."

They hug like old friends.

"So, you went and pissed off the wee wiseguy. Showed him up. This is his response. I've seen worse. Smart play might be to leave it at that."

When Kate doesn't answer, Emerson lets out a long breath.

Almost too quiet to hear, she says, "You know that's not how this started. You know what he did."

Doc takes one of the brooms and starts to sweep.

"Andrew, take the other broom."

He takes it from his mother. From the expression on his face, he is still digesting what his mother said. They all are.

Emerson too. "Daddy McMahon's been running things on this corner for a long time." He shrugs. "Maybe long enough. Just be careful who you put in the line of fire." The old cop looking right at Donovan when he says this.

"What a day," Kate says.

"I'll write this up. There'll be a record if you want to put in an insurance claim. Numb nuts is knocking on doors. We all know he won't get anybody on record. You take care, Kate."

"Thanks, Bobby."

"Didn't catch your name, soldier."

"Donovan."

"Sorry your visit wasn't a happier occasion. You knew Chris?"

"I did."

"Me and his dad were close. Dean Rogers was a little older'n me. Used to look out for me. Remember when Chris was born. Watched him grow up. His father was so proud. We all were. Hated to see him go off to war. Even worse seeing him come back."

He shakes out a Marlboro. Offers the pack to Donovan, who refuses. Soldiers, cops, firemen, they all smoke. Not worried about something that kills slowly, they see it happen too fast all their lives. Living that close to death, anything that takes the edge off is worth the price.

Emerson lights up and tastes the smoke like he probably does a lot of things, like it might be the last thing he'll ever do. "It's a fucked up world. Longer I live, more proof I see."

"I don't need any more convincing."

"I guess I don't either."

"Must be a tough town to be a cop in, Dorchester."

Emerson squeezes his eyelids, breathes a cloud of smoke out of his nose. "Just tough to be an honest cop. This is how it is. Anything happens outside of the store isn't self-defense. But don't plan on winning anything in the courts. They've got more judges and DA's and assistant DA's than they can keep track of. They've got alibis by the truckload."

"What do you suggest?"

"You really want to pursue this?"

"Let's say I do."

"Make it not worth it for them. Realize, for every guy you see, Nate, McMahon, there's a guy above him. Make it not worth it for them."

"Or just walk away." Donovan isn't sure if he's talking to himself or not.

"Course they'll be doing the same thing. Making it not worth it for you."

Donovan knew the rules of this game. Sean Connery's rules from "The Untouchables." He puts one of your men in the hospital, you put one of his in the morgue. The Chicago way. A head for an eye. This wasn't for some piece of the city's drug trade though. This wasn't a reprisal for one thug killing another, a non-sanctioned murder. This was a family trying to survive. What was that worth? I guess we'll find out, Donovan thinks.

Emerson and his partner canvas the neighborhood and leave.

They sweep up the glass. Kate finds some heavy curtains to hang in the window. Better than cardboard. A slight breeze makes the white sheets billow lazily, a soft whisper like laundry hung out to dry.

Nelson arrives with his kit, a foot locker's worth of guns and ammo. All filed of serial numbers. All well-oiled. They each take a pistol and holster. They smile at each other.

"Just like the old days," someone says. They are all thinking it.

Kate watches. She is not smiling. "This isn't just an excuse for you boys to play cops and robbers, is it?

His men look at him.

"Crash take the back. Billy, the front. Doc, me and you are second shift."

• • •

Later, Kate and Donovan are alone.

"Did you get Andrew to sleep?"

"What are you doing here, Patrick? Reliving the glory days?"

He taps his fake foot. "They weren't so glorious, Kate."

"I'm so tired of men getting killed around me. Tired of how it's just the way it is. Boys will be boys." She chokes back a sob, regains control. "Not my boy, Patrick."

He waits a moment, to be sure she's finished. He holds his arms out, embraces her. She shudders against his chest, weeps into his shoulder. He can't think of anything to say. All the dead bodies he's seen, the men he's killed, he has no wisdom to impart. He is tired of it too. They both know more men are going to be killed. Donovan knows who the first one will be. He is not sorry. But he's tired. Thinks, maybe, maybe, if things go right, this won't be the way it is. At least not here.

ELEVEN

—

KATE CAN'T SLEEP.

Keeps remembering the embrace. Patrick's strong arms, his solid chest. Her husband hasn't been in the ground a full day yet. Her mind can't stop undressing him, picturing him out of uniform.

Better to imagine that then how things might get worse. When word gets to Daddy O'Malley. What then? Will Patrick have a plan? Or will he be over his head? He seems so confident. Ready for anything. She wonders what his wound looks like. Without the prosthesis, she would like to see his scars. Would like to touch them.

Kate does the math of what a new window will cost. Less than their protection money certainly. Is it worth it?

Another question that will keep her up tonight, listening to the men, the soldiers, quietly patrol her home, her store. Wishing Donovan's footsteps would make their way to her bedroom door, to her bed.

She sighs. Rolls over. She's not dead yet. Her body is most definitely alive.

TWELVE

—

DONOVAN HAS A TRICK for sleeping light. He imagines himself on a tree branch, in his dream he is a boy. There are men after him. He must be silent. Has to listen for his pursuers. So he constantly jerks awake, thinks he is falling off that tree branch. Every noise in this strange house wakes him.

Doc is getting his fix on in the bathroom, something to last him until morning. Some of his mellow junk, stuff he can still function on, but still the room seems to throb, the colors go bright and dull, bright and dull, the objects in the room, the sink, the mirror, the toilet, swell and shrink, swell and shrink, like they're breathing. He exhales, an ecstatic release. Pain and fear are swallowed by what he thinks of as his shadow, he imagines the shadow of himself possessing him, his Mr. Hyde takes over, he gives in to his dark impulses, he could catch bullets with his teeth.

His habit began shortly after the incident at Kabul. When he was transferred to a new unit.

Fear. That was his bugaboo. He'd lost his swagger, that sense of immortality, suddenly he was fragile. Got the shakes, the kiss of death for a doctor. Needed something to make it stop, steady his nerves.

He found it. But he had it under control. Until he didn't.

That habit stuck to him, like a shadow. When he couldn't see it, it was eating him up from inside.

He could handle it. Quit when his tour was done.

But the habit followed him out of the service, into the real world, marriage, a kid. Still he couldn't give it up. What was he scared of now? His dreams, where the ones he couldn't save stared at him with black eyes. A tiny girl, shredded by bullets. The smack chased that girl away.

He zips up his works, licks his lips, savors that first rush. Tiptoes down the hall, through the kitchen.

The captain sits at a table in the dark. His eyes look right through Doc. "Better?"

"Yup."

Donovan nods, shrugs. He's looking out the window. "Nights are the worst, I think. Before I fall asleep. I know she'll be there. She's always there." He lifts a glass to his lips. Bourbon. He turns toward Doc. "Hey, I'm not the police and I'm not your father. We all do what we have to do. Right?"

"Right."

"So I'll just ask the one time. You okay?"

Doc lets out a sigh of relief. "I'm okay."

Donovan squints at him, not completely convinced but willing to let it slide. "Okay then. C'mon, we're on duty."

They relieve Crash and Nelson.

She visits the all in their sleep, as she has for years. For some reason, maybe the pistols within reach or the fact that they are all together again, the dreams are more vivid, her voice sings louder, they wake sadder.

The days creep.

Customers comment on the broken windows. The soldiers, in civilian clothes, try to be inconspicuous. In this neighborhood, strangers don't go unnoticed.

Donovan walks Andrew to school. A swarm of kids travels with them. The ones who weren't there want to know all about the fight. The ones who were there tell the tale. They embellish freely, shamelessly. Andrew takes Donovan's lead, doesn't talk more than he has to. Patrick can't help but grin.

"Back here at fifteen hundred hours, sharp."

"Yes, sir." A crooked smile, a lazy salute.

"Go learn something." Donovan doesn't remember until he's halfway back to the shop, that's what his father used to say to him and his brother every day before they left for school.

The nights are tense, the men antsy, Kate and

Andrew nervous, the reality of why they are there, why they are armed, is not discussed. Andrew watches the men clean their weapons, take them apart then reassemble them. But Kate has made it clear, the boy may not hold a weapon. They respect her wishes. Their firearms are kept holstered.

On the third or fourth night, a thought occurs to Donovan.

He goes downstairs to talk to the boys about taking a drive. To take the fight to Nate, instead of waiting for something to happen. Offense instead of defense.

THIRTEEN

—

CHRIS ROGERS HAUNTS NATE RILEY.

Nights in bars and pool halls, knocking back Budweiser long necks. Nate bullies his opponents, who know it isn't Nate who will do the fighting. One night, Nate breaks a cue over a young punk's head after losing to him three games in a row. Even for Nate, this is out of control behavior. He is desperate to intimidate people. Wants to see fear in people's eyes. Not like the soldier with the cane. Those mean, steel blue eyes. No fear there. Ever since that fucker did a number on his boy the neighborhood kids aren't treating him with the proper respect.

He can sense the whispering behind his back, knows the chuckles he hears are all directed at him. Just like back in school. By now the story of what happened has reached every grandma, every toddler and everyone in between.

The story, he's certain, has reached Daddy O'Malley.

Nate would like to go to the old man, ask for help, but pride won't let him. He needs to take care of this, himself, for him and the boys. And it needs to happen soon. He has to be cruel, something he normally enjoys, but not when it comes to Kate Rogers.

He wants to apologize, beg her for forgiveness. He had to do it. Chris would never have budged – even still, Nate would have let it slide, but Daddy O'Malley would have known. Would have replaced him. Is that what she wanted? Some stranger shaking them down. Some heartless punk from Southie who didn't give a shit who Kate Rogers was, who didn't know how special she was, how she needed to be protected.

Thoughts of Kate and Chris Rogers slosh in his head.

The combat zone whore sighs and says, "You want me to keep going, Shorty?"

His answer is the back of his hand.

FOURTEEN

DOC STAYS BEHIND. He knew somebody had to stay behind, knew why it was him, didn't like it, but agreed. After they leave, he prepares a special fix, to take the sting out of it.

They watch Nate come out of Aces High. Stumble more like it. A man followed by demons, Donovan thinks, a man trying to drink them away. Nate bumbles his way to his car, an old Chevelle. He spits on the sidewalk and slides in. The engine roars to life, on the radio, "Wayward Son" by Kansas.

Crash follows, not too worried about being spotted by the tipsy Nate.

"Looking for company, I'll wager," Donovan says. "And double or nothing says he has to pay for company."

Nate heads downtown. Stops at a strip club called

the Glass Slipper on La Grange for a few drinks, then creeps on foot to Chinatown.

Donovan and Billy follow. Observe from a distance as Nate negotiates with a spent street walker with cigarette-thin legs and a cough to match. She takes him around the corner to a sad motel that rents rooms by the hour.

Thirty minutes later, Nate storms out of the room, fuming, red-faced.

He never has a chance. It isn't a fair fight.

But is what happened to Chris Rogers fair? Did he ever have a chance? Donovan lets these questions comfort him as he pulls the wire tight around Nate's throat. He feels some satisfaction at the silence that descends on Nate, first his mouth, then his limbs, then his whole body goes quiet. The smell of his bowels releasing tells Donovan his victim is dead.

FIFTEEN

NATE DOESN'T KNOW what hit him. Just knows that he will never breathe again, his empty lungs scream in vain for air. The dim lights of the seedy motel go dimmer, he can't feel his legs. Then, a familiar face.

Chris Rogers. Not in a wheelchair. Standing. Young. The Chris Rogers who made him limp all the way to first base before he tagged him out.

His face is solemn. "Nate."

"What is this?"

The voice of a child. "I think it is hell."

SIXTEEN

NATE'S CAR IS FOUND in the morning with its windows smashed.

Parked in a metered spot, it is towed before nine. Donovan waits for the police to show up but nobody reports him missing for two days. His mother thinks it odd when he doesn't take the trash out for her on Wednesday, but it isn't the first time it's happened.

On Thursday, Frick and Frack retrace Nate's footsteps, place him at the Glass Slipper, then nothing. They check with the working girls but nobody's talking. If they knew any cops they might find out about Nate's car, but they don't, so they don't.

Friday morning, collection day, they go see Daddy O'Malley.

On Dorchester Avenue, a strange disquiet. The shop owners and tavern keepers all have their envelopes (or their excuses) ready. They wait for Nate and his flunkies to swagger through their doors, help themselves to a coffee or a beer. The merchants can already taste their swallowed pride. When nobody arrives they are pleased but nervous. They have no truck with optimism. Their rose-colored glasses were stomped on years ago.

As they go about their days they share secret glances with their neighbors. They look at the curtains in the corner store's shattered windows and wonder what happened.

Rumors scurry like mice.

Kate looks at Donovan and says, "What did you do?"

"Something that needed to be done."

"That's pretty vague, Patrick."

"It's nothing you need to know about."

Andrew is at school. Nelson walked him there. He'll stop for breakfast on the way back. Crash took the store's deposit to the bank. There is just enough cash in the store to operate with, not enough for their protection fee. Doc took the night shift, now he's sleeping in the room Donovan rented.

"What is it you think you're doing here, Patrick? Isn't there somewhere else you need to be?"

Donovan thinks of the sandy city of sin he calls home now. Knows there are probably a dozen messages from bad people. Dirty deeds that need doing. "I'm making sure nothing else happens to you."

She is close to him. No perfume, she smells like baby powder and apples, the scent from the shampoo he spied in her bathroom. "That's too bad. I was kind of hoping something might happen." Her eyebrows rise in a challenge.

"Don't do that."

"Do what?" Closer still.

Donovan's throat is dry, his body tingles. "I'm no saint."

"Good. I'm not looking for one."

The bell above the front door chimes.

Enter Daddy O'Malley.

Well dressed in a blue blazer, shirt and tie, khakis. His expensive loafers make soft, sharp taps on the tile floor. His head, as advertised, is completely bald, even his eyebrows are missing. His face is a scowl.

"Am I interrupting?" A deep voice, a Boston Irish brogue.

Donovan is surprised that he's alone, impressed.

When nobody answers, O'Malley's eyes scan the store. He nods at the front windows. "Shame about that." He clicks his tongue. "Shame about Chris, too, Kate."

"I got your flowers."

He narrows his eyes like a man who knows more than he's saying. "I can understand your feelings about

Nate. I'm not too happy with him either." O'Malley walks to the coffee bar, pours himself a small cup. "But I guess we don't have to worry about Nate anymore. Do we, Captain?"

Donovan keeps his poker face on.

"What's he talking about, Patrick?"

O'Malley grins at the revelation. A man who knows how to bluff.

"Nate's car was found downtown, near the old Combat Zone. What's left of it." He fingers the curtains in the front window, something like regret on his face. "All the windows were smashed in. No sign of young Nate. And I imagine Captain Patrick Donovan, former Special Forces, CIA spook, made him vanish without a trace."

Donovan avoids the look he knows is coming from Kate.

"So here we are. I'm missing a collection agent. I have a replacement in mind. You'll be seeing him around. But I'm willing to make a concession. You won't be seeing him in here."

"I've no interest in going toe to toe with you and your boys, Captain. No percentage in it. Win or lose, I lose. Too messy. Too much attention. So that's my offer. A generous one, I think. Please consider it. By all means, Butch, talk to the hole in the wall gang about it. Miss Kate, take care of that son of yours."

With a nod, almost a bow, Daddy O'Malley exits out the front door, graceful as a snake.

Something doesn't sit right with Donovan. He dials Crash's number.

They shoot Crash a block from the bank. A black Chrysler 300 pulls onto the sidewalk ahead of him, window down. Hits him in the center of the chest then peels away.

Doc, grooving to the beat of his heart, riding a wave of euphoria as the white powder surfs through his blood, senses something in his sleep. The door? Eyes closed he reaches for the Glock under his pillow when he feels the shots. One in the face, one in the chest.

Nelson waves to Andrew as the boy jogs into school. He breathes a sigh of relief, turns and feels the sting as he is hit in the gut. High pitched screams as he falls to his knees clutching his belly.

Paint balls. Circus clown red. All three men are covered in it. Welts on their skin where the balls hit and exploded. The pain on their bodies is nothing compared to the sting their pride felt. Daddy O'Malley's parting shot. They weren't even worth a bullet.

Doc is in the roughest shape, one eye swollen shut. When Donovan couldn't reach him by phone, he raced over in his rental car. Found him, moaning, holding his head, not sure what hit him. High as the moon and blind as a bat.

All three men are surprised to be alive and a little shook up. Donovan explains the situation. They are walking away. Mission accomplished. The crooks are off Kate's back. The man who killed Chris is dead. No reason for them to stay.

They know he's right.

They say their goodbyes to Kate.

Andrew doesn't want them to leave. Doc, Crash and Nelson, green berets, men who've seen things in battle that would send lesser souls to an asylum, who've killed more men than they can count, clear their throats, blink their eyes a little extra and give Andrew a hug, a pat on the head.

Outside the shop, Donovan shakes hands with each man. Not much to say but goodbye.

"See you in the next life, Cap," Nelson says.

All she has to do is say, stay, Donovan thinks. They look at him, mother and son. He knows he should leave. Knows it is too late for him. Or is it?

All she has to do is say, stay.

Andrew looks down at his shoes. "Are you leaving too?"

He wants to look at Kate, to read her expression. But what if she confirms what he knows? What if she knows it too? "Not just yet."

The hope in Andrew's eyes is like a drug Donovan would like to overdose on. He looks at Kate. Hope and hunger there.

"Let's get some food."

Kate changes quickly. Into a little black dress.

"Mom, you look good."

"Thanks, Andrew."

Donovan pats her down with his eyes.

"Hungry?" she says.

"Starving."

They walk to Angelo's Pizzeria. Red and white checkerboard tablecloths. Candles on top of Chianti bottles for light. Angelo comes out to greet them, kisses Kate, tries to pick up Andrew.

"You're too big now, boy. Man size." Angelo has a thick, Italian accent. A shrunken, olive-skinned man with a head of lustrous, snow white hair. He shakes hands with Donovan. "Ah, one of our guardian angels. A pleasure."

Donovan cringes on the inside, but smiles and returns the old man's vice grip.

He takes them to their table, doesn't give them menus. "I'm gonna whip you folks up something special."

They each have a glass of Valpolicella. Cheap but good, it suits the place. They toast.

"Thanks Patrick. For everything."

He shrugs. He didn't do much. Wonders, if he'd

never been born, would Chris be here with his family? Happy. Healthy.

The joint is crowded, festive, as if the neighborhood is exhaling. Munchkinland after Dorothy's house fell on the witch. Hard to remember who is sitting at which table because people keep moving, chatting with someone else.

Donovan remembers villages in Afghanistan, in Iraq, behaving like this. Grabbing a moment of joy, a night of celebration. Those beaten, miserable people knew how precious these moments were, how rare in their sad little lives. Just like these people. They had learned, the hard way, not to look too far down the road.

Kate arches an eyebrow in Donovan's direction. "Why so gloomy?"

"Hey, Patrick." Andrew is battling with a slice of pizza, as big as his head and thin as paper.

Donovan can't help but smile. "Yeah, kid?"

"When is it okay to get into a fight?"

You're asking the wrong guy, he thinks, searches for a safe answer. "I'm sure your mom would say, never."

Kate rolls her eyes.

"What do you say?"

Donovan bites his lip. "Someone takes a swing at you, Andrew, it is okay to defend yourself."

Andrew nods. "What if someone takes a swing at someone else? Someone smaller than them."

"Is something going on at school?" Kate says.

Andrew shakes his head, keeps looking at Donovan.

"It's okay to stick up for your friends, Andrew."

The boy's face is covered in sauce.

"It's also okay to get some of that pizza in your mouth."

A second bottle of wine arrives. Andrew's eyelids are heavy, his head nods. There is a friendly argument over payment. Angelo does not want their money. Donovan insists. A reverse shakedown.

Chris Rogers is not the only ghost watching Donovan and his widow and his son walk home. Whitey Bulger's victims are there; stool pigeons, witnesses, wise guys. They wander the streets of Dorchester from time to time. They see that nothing's changed. The big fish still eat the little fish. But this Donovan is tough to figure. He's upset the balance, for now. A tough guy with a conscience. So they watch, curious. If they still ran a book, they would take odds that Donovan's conscience will be his undoing.

Andrew sleepwalks through his bedtime rituals, unconscious as soon as his head hits the pillow.

Leaving just the two of them. And the ghost of Chris.

"I don't want to talk about it. How we shouldn't do

it. How it isn't right. How I just buried my husband. How it's wrong for Andrew."

She looks so goddamned beautiful, he can barely hear what she says over his pulse. Or is that her pulse? They are in her bedroom. A better man might care that this is where she slept with Chris but he's no saint.

"I don't want to talk about it," she says.

"So shut up."

It's been a while, for both of them. Close enough to smell each other. He tucks her hair behind her ear, his hand slides behind her neck pulls her to him. A low sound escapes her lips just before they meet his. They take their time, kiss with eyes open, taste each other, let their hands roam each other's backs. He slides his hands from her shoulders down her front, presses against her firm breasts, feels the push of her nipples through her shirt. She watches, mouth open, tongue sliding across her lips, eyes half closed. He pulls her shirt off. She removes her bra, slow and deliberate, her eyes on his, daring him to look down. He does and lets out a breath. She takes off her pants and stands for him in her panties.

"Your turn."

He lifts his arms as she yanks the shirt off of him. She kisses his neck, his chest, undoes his belt, pushes him onto the bed. When she starts to pull his pants down, he hesitates. "I want to see," she says. He relaxes. Once his pants are off, she touches his artificial leg. He shows her how to remove it, then chucks it across the room. They giggle.

She drinks in the sight of him. "So many scars."

He shrugs.

She starts with the white slash on his chin. A boyhood scar where his brother hit him with a hammer. She strokes it, kisses it. Does the same with all his scars, knife cuts, shrapnel wounds, she slides down his torso, both of them naked now, until she reaches his leg stump. She touches the shiny, grafted skin with both hands, with both lips, licks it. He moans from deep in his chest.

Then she pounces on him. A collision of lips and limbs, skin against skin. Hard and fast and breathless the first time. The second time begins as curious touching, an intimate exploration, their fingers linger here and there, then here again and again. Not too fast. Not yet.

Picture the ghost of Chris Rogers. Tortured, he sits on his old foot locker, abandoned in the corner of the bedroom. It holds his old uniforms, his government issued firearms. Kate doesn't know what to do with it, keeps it mainly for their son, in case he someday wants these things, these terrible reminders. Chris covers his eyes and ears but his transparent ghost hands hold nothing back. He sobs but in the real world his cries only sound like crickets. They could be as loud as freight trains, Kate and Donovan still wouldn't hear him. Nobody can now.

SEVENTEEN

—

IN THE MIDDLE OF THE NIGHT, Donovan becomes
aware of the ghost in the room. Guilt chews at his gut,
keeps him awake. He tries to let Kate's heavy breathing
soothe him back to sleep, but it's no use. Carefully, he
pulls himself up, hops to the corner where she threw
his leg. He fixes it in place and gets dressed. Watches
Kate sleep and thinks about getting back next to her.
Later, this will be his only regret, not returning to her
bed for one more embrace. He knows this but considers it his punishment. It seems to fit the crime.

Instead, he creeps downstairs. Out the broken front
window, Dorchester Avenue sleeps, the street lights
just blinking reds and yellows. He finds a chair and
sleeps with his eyes open, staring at the quiet scene
outside.

The neighborhood yawns to life. Cars become more
frequent. Donovan hears Kate's footsteps, but keeps

looking out the window. He tries, really tries, to picture himself staying. This would be his view. He tries to imagine it. Then feels Kate's hands on his shoulders, his neck, his face.

"Wasn't sure I'd find you."

He puts a hand on hers.

"Don't leave without saying goodbye."

He nods, still watches the street.

Kate flips the lights, unlocks the front door. "We are open for business."

"I think I'll buy a cup of coffee."

Donovan is still drinking the cup when he spots a man marching up the street. He knows it is O'Malley's new enforcer. Donovan stands in the front window when the man walks past. He casts a mean glance inside, meets Donovan's dead stare and turns away. He stalks, makes his way to Angelo's Restaurant. An easy, cowardly place to start. An old man. Donovan's whole body is tense, a coiled spring.

He isn't the only one watching.

From his bedroom window, Andrew sees the big man lumber into the restaurant. He opens the glass so he can hear. It is not long before the screams can be heard, the sounds of breaking dishes and furniture. No secrets on this street. Quiet everywhere else. The neighborhood listens. Andrew waits, for someone to do something, then realizes nobody will.

In his mother's room, his father's locker. He looks at the combination lock.

"Don't, Andrew," his father's ghost whispers in his ear.

The combination is his birthday. He flips open the lid. A khaki uniform, dog tags, a rifle, a pistol. The pistol, a dull gray the color of charcoal, sleek and sexy in his hand. He checks the clip like his father once taught him, like Donovan and his men do. He pops the clip back in place, puts a bullet in the chamber. More hollers from across the street.

Kate has a hand on Donovan's shoulder. His jaw is clamped shut so tight it hurts. His skin burns. O'Malley's man steps outside, spits on the sidewalk, tucks his shirt. Donovan's fingers dig into his palms.

Andrew is a blur as he runs across the street.

Two hands point the pistol at the street.

"Jesus Christ," Kate says.

She bolts out of the store. Donovan limps after her.

Neither is fast enough.

The gun, now raised, pulls Andrew like a divining rod.

He is six feet away when the hulk of a man notices the boy. Says, "What's that you got there, kid?"

A commotion in his head, in his chest, of heart beats and the voices of his mom, Donovan, the gangster in the black leather cowboy boots, cars honking, his father.

His father? Andrew swears he can hear him whisper, "Don't miss, son."

And the gun, not heavy anymore, so light he thinks it might float out of his hands, he pictures the bullets, snug in the chamber, anxious to fly, making his whole body itch.

Then all he can hear is the pistol barking.

The bullets punch holes in the man.

The scent of gunpowder and blood fills his nostrils.

Then the gun does fly out of his hands. No. His mother rips it away from him. He never realized how strong her hands were before. She is shrieking and crying, but these are the deaf seconds after gunshots and he can't hear her. Can only watch the life ooze out of the man he shot. The thug's eyes twitch, look everywhere for an escape, his hands move from wound to wound, too much blood to stop, then his dark eyes seem to lock on something far away, coming closer.

Until everything about the man is still.

I did this, he thinks. I killed you. Like somebody killed my dad.

Donovan puts a finger to the man's throat. No pulse. He shakes his head at Kate. Andrew notices. "It's okay to stick up for my friends. Right, Patrick?"

Donovan closes his eyes.

The dead man watches them with his dead eyes.

"Nothing that just happened is okay, Andrew," Kate says.

Donovan opens his eyes to look at the confused boy.

"Why?" the boy wants to know.

"How can you ask that?"

"He was a bad guy."

Donovan stands, finds a piece of scrap paper in his wallet, writes something on it.

"He was a bad guy," Kate says. "I don't want you to have to turn into a bad guy."

Donovan clears his throat. "Kate, you both need to get out of here. He hands the piece of paper to her. "Pack a bag. Take the car. I'll meet you here as soon as I can."

"Where is this?"

"Vermont. A hotel."

"What?"

"In the town I grew up in. Nobody will look for you there. I'll stay and clean this up."

She holds the paper in her fist.

He pulls the boy close, hands on Andrew's shoulders. "Take care of your mom. Go with her and protect her."

"Am I a bad guy, Patrick?"

"No, kid. I am. Go pack your stuff."

When the boy turns to cross the street, Donovan

grabs Kate and kisses her roughly. "Get out of here. I'll meet you there. Go."

In the distance, a bird call of sirens flies closer.

EIGHTEEN

—

ANDREW DOESN'T OFTEN LEAVE his neighborhood. Takes a trip to the Cape once a year, splashes in the ocean. The numbers of the roads, 128, 95, mean nothing to him, he has never been out of the state before. Strange watching the buildings get farther and farther apart. Trees invade the landscape, an army of green. Until there is only forest and the uncrowded road, strange to drive so fast. And the mountains. The boy feels dizzy, slightly nauseous. From the speed, or the height, or agoraphobia, or the adrenaline recently pumping through his heart, who knows.

His senses are overwhelmed by what he just did. The blood so red, the smell of it still in his nose, the sound of the gunshots the loudest thing he has ever heard, the weight of the pistol in his hand, too heavy to be a toy. He shivers, tries to swallow the dirty penny taste in his mouth.

•   •   •

Kate is a jangle of raw nerves.

She has never been this far north. Nothing is familiar, everything disorients her. When they finally get onto 91, although they climb straight north, it feels like they are traveling in circles, passing the same towns and houses. The only things that change are the numbers on the exit signs that slowly, slowly climb.

Mountains everywhere. She wonders how anything could be straight in this land. She is afraid she will be always rolling downhill, or trudging uphill. Everyone must be tired all the time, always aware of gravity.

Route 100 is a narrow, two-lane road that serpents around or over mountains, there are few straightaways in Vermont with all these hills to dodge.

Eventually they come to the Green Mountain Motor Lodge, the property chopped out of the forest, a long, narrow, brown building. An old man – who talks just like the old Pepperidge Farm guy – is happy to take cash for the room.

The air. Crisp and cold. Clean, that's the difference. Not polluted with gas fumes and the scents of dozens of restaurants. There are two Adirondack chairs outside their room. Mother and son sit, take in the view, and breathe that mountain air.

•   •   •

The gun. First, Donovan needed to lose the gun. It's at the bottom of the Charles now. The easiest thing he will do today.

Daddy O'Malley is not a difficult man to find. He is a neighborhood boss who likes his presence to be felt. Afternoons he can be found at the corner of Dot Avenue and Park Street at Lucky's Pub, shooting pool. His game is straight pool. His father was a pool shark and taught his son everything he knew. All the angles. On and off the table. Lessons that have served him well.

His crew members would let him win, but they never need to. O'Malley's bag of tricks is legendary. Sometimes, when his cronies are tired of losing to him, he will show off some English, make the cue ball stop on a dime or spin like a top around the felt.

Today, two men stand guard outside the front door, Billy and Chris Shea, Irish twins, eleven months apart. Spawned from a long list of thugs, they both have huge, mean, blue eyes in a perpetual scowl, skin the color of cement. .45's hide under long leather coats. Their fat heads sit atop necks the size of telephone poles.

Their standing orders are to let nobody in they don't know. No exceptions.

From his rental car, Donovan sees them standing on the sidewalk, exuding ill will.

He steps on the gas. Thirty five miles per hour. Forty.

Swerves over the curb.

Gets lucky, crushes them both against the front wall. It is an agonizing way to die. They don't go quietly.

Donovan shoots the glass out of the large front window. The sounds of shattering glass and bullets join the screams of the dying brothers. For Donovan, it is just the familiar noises of war. He does not have time for plans or subtlety. No time to smoke O'Malley out and wait for him to try to escape. He must charge into the lion's mouth, the belly of the beast.

O'Malley's crew doesn't know what is happening, like animals with no natural predator they have grown lazy and careless. Some of them assume it is a car accident, at first, some drunk on a bender. That must be it.

"Did you hear gunshots?"

A few look to O'Malley.

"Check it out."

No need. Donovan rushes in through the jagged, gaping hole where the window was, double fisting .38 caliber pistols. O'Malley watches the heads of his crew members explode. The few that are not hit get the hell out the back door.

O'Malley still stands at the pool table, cue in hand.

Donovan levels his pistol at the fat man. Quiet infiltrates the pub. O'Malley studies the table, looking for a shot.

"I spent a lot of time in pool halls as a kid." He lines up a shot, drops the six in the corner. "That was pretty much how my dad made a living, so if I wanted to see him…" O'Malley glides to a spot as the white ball stops right in front of him. "He always said, 'Don't take a guy's last dollar. Just take everything else.' Three in the side." He nails it. Chalks his stick. He runs the table, graceful as a dancer, calls his shots.

One ball left.

O'Malley sighs, then leans over the shot. Hits the ball low, making it hop off the table, launch at Donovan's head. He squeezes the trigger, the ball bursts, the bullet continues into O'Malley's chest.

He leaves out the back door, ready for trouble but none waits for him there.

NINETEEN

O'MALLEY'S DEATH IS BIG NEWS, an old school, old guard mobster taken out in broad daylight. A daring lone gunman. This is bad for business, bad publicity. The bosses in Providence kick it upstairs, to New York. Cosa Nostra needs to know that they've lost a neighborhood.

Giovanni Junior tries to get his head around it. How does this happen? The brazenness of the attack. He makes inquiries. Sends some men to talk to some people. He wants information, he wants somebody's head. Misses the good old days. Something doesn't figure. O'Malley was a god boss. Knew his neighborhood, grew up there. Knew how to handle things, how to keep a low profile. Some foreign presence is at work here. An x-factor.

Yes, his sources confirm, soldiers, in town for a funeral.

What soldiers?

Some bad ass Special Forces soldiers.

Like the fucking A-Team? Who?

Nobody knows who. The only ones who would know are gone. A woman, a shop owner and her son.

Tell me about the soldiers, Junior says. Who was their leader?

Maybe forty. Walked with a cane.

Giovanni feels a chill shiver up his spine.

A cane?

Maybe missing a foot is what we heard.

Silver? No. But that could explain it. A man with balls the size of cantaloupes. But why? Giovanni tries to think back to Vegas, to the conversation between Alejandro and Silver. Silver knew the rules. A mercenary, yes, but a solid criminal citizen. Loyal to his employers. This makes no sense.

Johnny Silver gone rogue is a serious problem. The Dorchester situation is a disaster. Giovanni sighs. A serious problem requires a serious solution. He reaches out to his favorite problem solver.

Alejandro Poma.

Alejandro is courting in Mexico. Not for a bride, though he is talking to a woman. They need a new distributor to replace the one Alejandro eliminated, José. He is in the company of Rosa Escondido, Reya of the Sonoran Desert.

They know each other by reputation only. Rosa's beauty has been legendary since she was a teenager. She is exquisite in person. The face of a madonna, he was told, and a figure for the devil.

He is not prepared for her eyes, so dark they appear black. They reveal a toughness he hadn't expected. Never underestimate, he chides himself.

"Why me?" she asks.

He suspects that she knows. "*La verdad*?"

She narrows her big, bad eyes. "Yes, the truth."

He grins. "You are hungry. Since your father passed, rest his soul, your operation has shrunk. Your competitors sensed weakness."

"They were wrong." A sentence delivered on ice.

He knows. Knows all about the dead cartel chiefs. "We agree, Señora Escondido. That is why I am here."

She appreciates that he has come in person. Alejandro Poma. The Colombian Killer. Could have sent one of his minions. He is more handsome than she expected, thinner, prettier. He should be in Hollywood, she thinks. An actor or a singer. He has cheekbones to die for and a seductive baritone voice.

He is more playful than she expected. She's known killers, been around them all her life. But this one is playful, a flirt. It disarms her. He doesn't carry the ghosts of his victims around like other killers she's known.

Like Patrick Donovan.

She heard Donovan was involved with the elimination of José Saucedo. In Vegas, supposedly. Just disappeared. Nothing left but rumors. Not that she's complaining.

Alejandro is waiting for an answer.

"The volume you're talking about would be difficult to distribute."

He shrugs, flashes his perfect grin. "We could help with that."

"Really?"

"If you like. We know a man in New York who might be interested."

She chuckles. He is trying hard for nonchalance. A man in New York can only mean Giovanni Junior. And to mention him means this was his idea. She is flattered.

"Please tell Señor Giovanni that I think we can work something out."

His smile gets bigger. Beauty and brains. Very good.

Then his phone rings. The tone is Sinatra. *New York, New York.*

"El hombre de Nueva York?" she says.

"May I?"

"Of course."

It is a one sided conversation.

"Very well." He hangs up.

"*Una problema?*"

"Yes." Then he remembers. There's a connection here. "Maybe a problem you can help with."

"Really?"

"We're looking for a man I think you know. A man who walks with a cane. I believe he worked for your father some years ago."

He sees the recognition in her eyes which have suddenly gone soft.

"This was a while back. Maybe you were too young to remember. But you might. He was an American. Made quite a name for himself."

Her eyes smolder now. Something serious between them.

"Why are you looking for him?"

"He has caused quite a disturbance in one of our neighborhoods in Boston."

She bites her lip to keep from smiling. Patrick. Still raising hell.

"And now he has vanished. Do you know where we might find him?"

"I might."

"Can you tell me? El hombre de Nueva York would be most grateful."

"No. But I can show you."

TWENTY

—

CRASH SEES IT ON THE NEWS. Recognizes the street, Kate's shop. Sees the police tape where the body was on the sidewalk. No witnesses. Man with suspected mob ties. What the hell happened? He'll have to go find out. He repacks his bag. Hits the road back to Boston.

Doc is deep in the land of nod, miles beneath the surface of the world, nearly weightless, enveloped, untouchable. Until the voices start. Something he thought was long dead is sore. His pride. Who knew? Chased out of town by some local thug. He remembers the bad trip of that paintball to his face. A point blank shot at his ego. *And the man who ordered it still walking around, laughing at how he made us run*, Doc thinks. It won't do. It's messing with his high, harshing his mellow.

He opens his foot locker. Pulls out his old service

revolver. *Hello, old friend.* He holds its familiar weight. Takes it apart, oils it, puts it back together, loads it. *We are not quite finished with each other.*

The phone rings. Crash.

"I'm on my way."

Nothing has changed in Nelson's bar. He wonders if the barflies on their usual stools have even left since he's been gone. Out the window facing west, thunderheads loom, an avalanche of clouds wrecking the perfect blue in its path, wind kicks dust ahead of it. He pours himself a shot of Beam, opens a Lone Star bottle. Sips one, then the other. Finds his reflection in the mirror behind the bar. He's just another old and worn part of the room.

"How was the trip?" His bartender, Dale, runs things in his absence.

Nelson finishes the whiskey, winces, chases the sting with the beer.

"Some folks been looking for you."

The usual suspects no doubt. Looking for something to help them kill someone.

"Told 'em you'd be back afore long."

Nelson takes his beer and his duffel bag to the apartment he keeps above the bar. A simple, spartan place. Bed, chair, couch, kitchen table with four chairs. He unpacks his dirty clothes, places them in the hamper. Then packs some fresh clothes.

He finishes his beer but it does nothing to wash the

bad taste out of his mouth, the taste of defeat. He'd forgotten what it tasted like. That's why he lets others do the fighting now. Can't lose if you don't play. He runs cold water in the sink, splashes some on his face. Tries to tell himself it doesn't matter. He's repaid his debt. The mother and her son in Boston are safe. Kate and Andrew are safe. Aren't they? The only thing hurt was Nelson's pride. Tells himself he'd simply walked away. But he looks into his eyes and knows the truth. He's been chased away.

Can he live with that?

The clouds billow closer, the wind picks up. The blue sky runs away. Nelson walks downstairs with his newly packed duffel bag.

Dale eyes it. "When will you be back?"

"Don't wait up."

It's all over the news. Even in Vermont. Kate wishes Andrew wasn't listening, but she needs to know what happened. They keep referring to an 'unidentified assailant.' No police sketch. No apparent witnesses.

Reputed mob boss, David O'Malley dead. Pub turned into a shooting gallery. Ten dead men. She shivers. Didn't realize what Patrick was capable of. She hates the pride in her son's wide eyes. The two men she loves now. Killers.

But she knows why he did it. For her. For Andrew.

For all the right reasons. She thinks of the road to hell and its pavement.

What now? She has trouble imagining the Dot without Daddy O'Malley. Will there be a new boss? Same as the old boss?

Maybe it's time for someplace new. A place with no bosses, where guns aren't as common as one way streets in Boston. Does such a place exist? Is she there now?

Her head spins so fast she has to lie down.

They sit outside on the chairs, watch the sunset. The thin air makes them tired and hungry.

A black sedan with Massachusetts plates pulls into the lot. Drives toward them, parks next to their car. Patrick at the wheel. He steps out, walks to where they sit. His expression heavy. Kate wants to embrace him, pepper his neck with kisses, but she is aware of her watchful son.

Andrew is excited, starts to blurt something, but Patrick holds up a hand, a finger to his lips. Andrew nods.

She wonders what life would be like with him. Is it worth finding out? Wonders how old he is. Forty?

He leads them both inside.

"Is it over?" she says.

He looks at her with hangman's eyes. "Maybe. We're gonna wait up here until things cool down. Make sure the cops aren't looking for Andrew."

"What if they are?" the boy asks.

Patrick's voice turns kind. "I'd be surprised. I don't think anyone from the neighborhood will talk. And you need to do likewise."

"What's likewise?"

"You shooting that guy? That never happened. You don't talk about it. Not with the kids in the neighborhood. Not with your girlfriend. Not even with Angelo. You want to talk to your mom about it, just make sure nobody's within a mile of you."

Andrew nods looking at the carpet.

Kate cannot take her eyes off Patrick. The need to touch him causes a low pain in her stomach.

"Look at me, Andrew."

Patrick's eyes are steel.

"I ever hear about you playing with guns, wherever I am, I will track you down and beat the shit out of you."

A small smile crosses the boy's lips.

"I'd do it now for all the trouble you caused if it wasn't for how goddamned brave it was."

Andrew laughs, then yawns.

"Tired, kid?"

The boy nods.

"Me too. We all had a long day. And this mountain air always does a number on me. Let's hit the hay. I'm gonna go get my own room."

The boy is asleep in minutes, his breathing heavy and steady.

Kate feels terrible about leaving him, but she needs to be touched, needs some friction against her skin. He is outside his room in a chair, a bottle of Maker's Mark on the ground, a half full glass in his hand.

"Need a drink?"

"Sure."

He pours a few fingers into an empty glass.

She savors the burn that spreads from her lips, down her throat to her gut. Takes another sip. "That's not all I need." She takes his glass, puts it and hers on the ground, sits on his lap. As they kiss, they stare at each other, his lips delicious with the taste of bourbon, his face rough with stubble.

Then she stops. Stands and picks up her drink. He follows her lead.

When they are naked on his bed, she asks, "What do you want?"

He wants to be so deep inside her he forgets his name, how many people he's killed, watched die, forgets where he's from or why he's here, so deep that all he can think of is this young body, this perfect skin, moist with perspiration.

As if she can hear his thoughts, "Then do it already."

It begins as a hard embrace, pressed against each other, as though she is completely wrapped around him. Sounds of longing escape their lips. Slowly, they begin to move, a building rhythm, below the waist, faster, then faster, harder and harder. Their mouths, between kisses, spit out ecstatic nonsense. They don't want it to end, but they can't wait to feel that crowning sensation. They race, children running down a hill, out of control, until the ground levels off and they fall, breathless and giddy.

"I have to go back to my room."

"I know." His hand wanders down her back.

"I don't want to."

"You need to."

"You could come." She is on her stomach, head on her arms. She looks out the window.

"I don't know if I should."

"I don't either." She can't separate her wants and needs. Tries to trace her recent past, to put her finger on the point of no return. Did it happen in the past week? Or was it something much earlier? An event years ago that doomed her to this fate.

"None of this is your fault."

She gets up.

He watches her dress. Takes mental snapshots in case he has to leave in a hurry, in case he never sees her again. He wonders how much of this is his fault. Would the boy ever have had the thought of using that pistol without Donovan's influence? Maybe.

"It's a bad world. He was trying to do something good."

"Do you think he did something good?"

"He killed a bad man. He stood up to a bully."

"Like his father."

As if invoked, Donovan sees the ghost of Chris Rogers. "I saved your life," the ghost hisses. "This is how you repay me?" He cannot look the ghost in the eye.

Before she leaves, she kisses him on the cheek.

He pours two drinks. One for him. One for Chris. Knocks his glass against Chris's. "Here's mud in your eye."

"What's the plan, Captain?"

Donovan examines the contents of his glass, take a sip.

"Stay up here, live like Ozzie and Harriet? Introduce her to the family?"

Was that the plan?

Chris sips his bourbon. "What you don't realize yet, soldier, is that you haven't paid for your sins. Sooner or later we all pay for them."

Donovan looks out into the night. The familiar Vermont darkness of his childhood. When he turns back, the young girl has taken Chris's place.

"I'm trying to pay for them."

He wonders why she looks so sad. Because of what happened to her, or what will happen to him? What he wouldn't do to see her smile.

She stands. Walks to him. Her tiny feet are bare.

This world is no place for children, he thinks. She pulls him to her, kisses him on the lips. She taste like whiskey and tears.

TWENTY-ONE

—

LEAVES ON THE TURN. Red and orange and yellow explosions amidst a few stubborn greens. Everything on a slant. The small sky squeezed between the mountains. No straight roads, they twist and turn, always going up or down. A land of flannel and denim, chimney smoke and rotting leaves.

Home.

His senses come alive, aware of every familiar sight, sound or smell. And the memories come barreling out of the back of his head.

"Where are we?" Andrew asks.

"This is where I grew up."

"Seriously?"

"Seriously."

His elementary school, the field where he played little league baseball, where he hit his first home run. The apple orchard where he kissed his first girl. What was her name? Sara. Sara Banks. Blonde and blue-eyed, cheeks full of freckles. Then old man Byron had chased them off his property, thinking they were stealing apples. Such a small world he'd lived in. When you got in trouble with the cops they didn't bring you to jail, they brought you home. Let your parents punish you. Donovan remembered a lot of drives home in the back of Chief Tyson's cruiser. Sometimes with two or three others. He'd drop all of them off, one by one. His mother's tears. His father's quick back hand to Donovan's temple.

"Did he kill anybody?" his father would ask.

"Not tonight."

"When are you gonna smarten up, kid?"

When indeed?

Donovan feels the same tightness in his chest that he felt as a teenage boy, coming home past curfew, as he pulls into his parents' driveway. The same post and beam log cabin waits for him. Some of his earliest memories are his father and dozens of his friends building the house. The smell of wood, the sound of hammers everywhere, even his dreams. When they reach the end of the long driveway, a black Labrador Retriever, his father has always owned one, who knows how many this makes, runs out to greet them, jumping and barking.

Donovan parks next to his father's Chevy pickup. He gets out first and pets the dog. "Who's a good dog?"

"Well, look what the cat dragged in." Exactly what his mother used to say when the cops dropped him home in high school.

She is thin, too thin, like always. Limbs made of sticks. Her hair short and gray now, but still stylish. Kind blue eyes in a pretty, smiling face. A denim jacket over a blue sweater. Khaki pants, gray sneakers.

"I half expected you two characters to have flown south for good by now."

The dog tries to jump on Donovan.

"Smedley, down."

His mother walks gingerly down the steps from the kitchen and hugs her boy.

"Speaking of characters, who's in the car?"

Donovan motions for Kate and Andrew to get out of the car. They do, wearing sheepish grins.

"Mom, this is Kate and her son, Andrew. Guys, this is my mom, Olivia Donovan."

Kate and his mother shake hands. Mrs. Donovan pats Andrew on the head. "A handsome boy."

"Thank you, Mrs. Donovan."

"Please, call me Olivia. What brings you folks up north?"

Donovan is saved from lying, at least for a moment, by the appearance of his father. Tall and rugged, dressed in flannel and denim, a few days growth on his face, he comes out of the kitchen door looking like a gray haired Paul Bunyan. "Fee fi fo fum," he whispers,

"I smell the blood of Patrick Donovan." His voice startles, higher than one would expect. Disarming.

"Hey, Pops."

"Hi, son."

They embrace. His father smells like the woods, like pine trees and wood smoke.

"And visitors."

"Kate, Andrew, my dad, Robert Donovan."

"Bob, please. One 'O'." His oldest joke. Andrew cracks up when he gets it. Bob shakes both their hands. "Welcome to our humble abode. Please come inside."

His mother puts on a cup of coffee. The linoleum floor has been replaced with tile, the old kitchen table shrunk to fit only two. The wallpaper is the same, a duck pattern, mallards and cinnamon teals and northern pintails, silhouetted in flight. It smells the same, like coffee and maple syrup and bacon. The familiar surroundings relax Donovan.

When Kate tells them were they are from, he sees his father's pale blue eyes narrow. His mother comments on the bad news coming out of Boston lately. "Are you near Dorchester?"

Andrew's eyes go wide but he bites his tongue.

"Not far," Kate says.

Mrs. Donovan asks, "Where were you planning on staying?"

"Over at the Echo Lake Inn," Patrick says.

"We've got plenty of room here, Patrick," his mother says.

Mr. Donovan nods.

"We wouldn't want to impose," Kate says.

"Nonsense," Mr. Donovan says.

"Be a treat to have some company."

"Well, thanks," Patrick says. "That'd be nice."

"You remember how to split wood, son?"

"Like riding a bicycle, isn't it?"

"I just got a cord dropped off. Be lying if I said I couldn't use a hand."

Donovan rubs his hands together. "Let us grab our bags and I'll grab an axe."

He borrows some work clothes from his dad. A thermal, long sleeve t-shirt, some boots, gloves. He stretches like his father taught him twenty or thirty years ago. Takes a few swings with the axe like a baseball player in the on deck circle.

Then they get to work. The sounds of heavy breathing, of steel splitting wood, are as familiar to Donovan as the sound of crickets at night in the summer. His father's long limbs are as powerful and his axe stroke as graceful as ever. Once Patrick's joints loosen, he finds his old rhythm.

"How bad is it?" his father asks.

"Pretty bad."

"Anything we can do?"

"You're doing it."

"You know what you're doing?"

"I'm splitting wood."

His father bites his lower lip. Rubs his shoulder. "I guess there's worse things you could be doing."

After a while, Andrew wanders out.

"How goes it, Andrew?" Patrick asks.

"Your mom keeps trying to feed me."

The men grin.

"That's what she does when she doesn't know what to do."

"Can I help?" the boy asks.

Bob examines the boy. "Ever use an axe before?"

"Nope."

"How old are you?"

"I'll be eleven in March."

"I guess it's about time you learned to swing an axe."

Andrew's face blooms with excitement.

Bob holds his axe out to the boy.

Patrick knows what's coming.

"Touch the blade with your thumb, son."

Hesitantly, Andrew touches it. He cuts himself and drops the blade. "Ow."

"Okay." Bob picks up the handle and holds it out for Andrew. "Imagine how much damage that blade could do if it was moving. That's the last time I want that blade to touch any part of you."

Andrew's thumb in in his mouth. He looks at the blade suspiciously, looks at Patrick.

"He's done playing tricks on you, Andrew. Did the same thing to me when I was your age." Donovan goes to the shed and finds a pair of gloves for the boy.

"Sorry, son. Some lessons you need to learn the hard way."

"Andrew knows all about hard lessons, dad."

"Show him how it's done, Patrick."

Donovan sets up a piece of wood. With a smooth motion he splits it.

"No need to swing for the fences, Andrew. Just a nice, smooth stroke. Try it without any wood there."

Awkwardly, Andrew raises and swings the axe.

"Choke up a little."

A better swing this time.

"Let the blade do some of the work."

Better still.

"Sure you never did this before?"

Pride in the boy's eyes.

"Now aim it. Right at the center of the stump."

Close.

"How'd that feel?"

"Good."

"Let's set up some wood."

His father always believed in the value of manual labor, not just for the body, but the mind as well. That it was possible to achieve a sort of Zen meditation. Andrew soon gets lost in the task, finds his own rhythm. The split wood starts to pile up. Father and son look at each other and nod. It was the same pre-scription for Patrick when he was young. When he was pining for some girl or cooling off after a fight. Splitting wood had always soothed his nerves. He is relieved to discover it still does.

Andrew does well, but tires quickly, the blade gets trapped more and more, so they stop.

The day has warmed up now but a slight breeze cools off their sore, sweaty bodies.

They head inside where Mrs. Donovan has pre-pared ham sandwiches. Spiral ham cut off the bone and thick slices of bread from the Sweet Surrender Bakery in town. The boys devour their food.

After lunch, the men stack wood in the garage. Donovan finishes chopping the remainder of the cord.

Smedley watches them work. The boy and the dog become fast friends. When the wood is stacked neatly, Bob suggests that Andrew take him for a walk.

"Just don't go past the pond," he says.

Off they go.

Donovan watches with a smile. Remembers the hours he spent in those woods as a child. Wonders if this city boy has ever spent any time in the woods with a dog.

"Thanks, son. You and Andrew have saved my back a lot of aggravation."

"Happy to help."

Kate and his mother pull into the driveway, back

from the store with dinner supplies. Mrs. Donovan rolls down her window.

"I spoke to your brother. He's coming by for dinner."

"The more the merrier."

Not long before the boy and the dog are deep in the woods. Smedley leads Andrew along a trail that climbs over a ridge, then down to a clearing next to a pond. The still water is a mirror of the fall colors. Andrew's muscles are sore from splitting wood, but it feels good, a satisfaction from accomplishing a difficult task accompanies the aches. Offsets it.

Smedley notices the woman first. A change in the wind reveals her scent. Reminds Andrew of the smell of flowers at his father's wake. The dog moves in for closer inspection. She stands at the edge of the water, arms folded. When Smedley gets close enough, she bends and pats him.

"And who might you two be?" She has an accent, pronounces *you* like *jew*. Her skin is dark, the color of his mother's coffee. She wears jeans and a purple fleece jacket. Midnight colored hair spills from under a puffy white hat. Dark eyes look at Andrew from a face so beautiful it renders him speechless. She turns to the dog.

"He doesn't seem very talkative. Maybe you could tell me his name."

She scratches behind the dog's ears. The animal

makes ecstatic noises. Andrew would like to trade places.

"What's that?" She leans close, looks over at the boy. "Andrew? Yes, he looks like an Andrew."

This does nothing to help Andrew's powers of speech. Is this really happening?

"What? You never met a lady could talk to animals?"

"No."

"Ah." She smiles. "He does speak."

He feels his face blush.

"But you don't know my name. How rude of me. My name is Rosa."

A gust of wind and Rosa shivers. The clothes she wears look brand new, as though purchased just for this trip.

"Do you live around here?" he asks.

"Do I look like I live around here?"

"No."

She looks like the queen of some lost city, a Latin Cleopatra. Rosa squints at him. "You're in a lot of trouble, Andrew. With some very bad men."

"How do you know that?"

She leans close to his face, he can find no flaw on hers. "Tell me I'm wrong."

He looks at his feet.

She nods. "It is very important that I talk to Patrick, Andrew. *Muy importante* for you and your mother. Do you understand?"

Andrew nods.

A man appears out of the woods, without making a sound, dark haired, dark skinned, dark eyed. Offers Rosa a quizzical look.

"*Es el chico?*"

"*Sí.*"

The man turns his terrible eyes on Andrew. A face carved out of wood, hard as oak. No expression. The dog growls at him. The man growls back.

"Tell Patrick we need to see him, Andrew. But don't tell your mother. Tell him to hurry. I don't know how long I can stand this cold."

At these words, Andrew shivers. He lets the dog pull him back towards the house. When he looks back at her, Rosa blows him a kiss.

The boy looks spooked. By what he's done? Is it finally sinking in? Or did something happen out in the woods? Donovan scans the trees for silhouettes as he considers, stacking wood at the same time.

Andrew comes close, voice hushed. "There was a woman at the pond."

"A woman?"

"Rosa. She said she knows you. Said we were in a lot of trouble. With some bad guys."

He searches the woods harder now. Rosa Escondido. You are far from home, young lady. Not quite as young as you used to be. Rosa. Now the head of the Escondido Cartel. Here to pay back a favor? Or solve a problem?

"Did she have anybody with her?"

"I saw one man. She said she needs to talk with you."

"Did she now?"

"Yup."

Donovan closes his eyes, lets out a long breath. Tries to picture her. It's been years.

The boy is scared. "What should we do?"

He squeezes Andrew's shoulder. "I think I should go talk to my old friend, Rosa."

"Can I come?"

"I don't think so. Can you stack the rest of this wood for me?"

"Sure."

"Don't worry. I'll be back soon."

He can see in Andrew's eyes that telling him not to worry would only tell him there is something to worry about.

Not as easy to walk through the woods as it used to be. His peg leg cannot make the sudden changes needed to avoid the roots and rocks that keep trying to trip him. He takes it slow. Thinks of Rosa. The reason he left Mexico.

He had watched her grow, from teenager into young womanhood. She had shed her teen chubbiness and turned into a knockout. A nightmare for her father, constantly worried about the thugs he employed, who weren't blind after all. After a few beatings by Escondido for a few sideways glances at his daughter, it was understood the girl was off limits. The few boys from school who were brought home, upon entering the hacienda were introduced to Escondido's gun rack. Not a subtle display.

Not that any of this mattered.

She only had eyes for Donovan.

He was the reason she begged her father for a treadmill, the reason she starved herself.

It seemed, to Donovan, like a harmless crush at first. He chuckled about it. When she asked him what he thought about her new bikini, her new skirt – was it too short? He avoided looking at her. Gave her short replies. Very nice. It's fine. Rosa's mother teased her about falling for the gringo.

In time, Donovan realized the danger of this attraction, the likely consequences of acting on it. But in those days, every day was dangerous. Like being back at war, he was in enemy territory, a conqueror among the natives, so the attention of an eighteen year old girl was the least hazardous thing on his plate.

Then she came to his bedroom. In the middle of the night.

"Who saw you come in here?"

"Nobody."

"Rosa, go back to bed."

"What if someone sees me leave?"

"Are you trying to get me killed?"

"No, Patrick. That's not what I'm trying to do."

She stood next to his bed in a silk robe. Slowly, her delicate hands untied it. It opened to reveal her tan skin. She was tall now and slender with wide shoulders. The shape of her firm, young breasts made his stomach flutter.

"Rosa, please go back to your room."

As if a strong breeze had blown through the room, her robe slid off her shoulders, fell to the floor in a splash of silk.

"Patrick, I know you. Who you are, what you are. A killer."

She was at the edge of the bed now.

"I don't care. I want you."

She smelled like vanilla and honey.

"Don't you want me?"

Her mouth tasted like sangria, sweet, intoxicating. Her body, long and lean and limber, was a Stradivarius, perfectly tuned, responding to the slightest touch with a melodious cantilena.

Of all his many mistakes, this was his favorite.

There she is. By the pond. Older but no less beautiful. Maybe more. Her eyes possess a touch of tragedy now, a hint of meanness. She's had to bury a few bodies to stay where she is. And it agrees with her.

She smiles at him, shivers a little. "Patrick."

"Rosa."

"Long time."

He is aware of a man, hers no doubt, observing from the woods. "What brings you to the north country?"

"A lot of people are looking for you."

"That right?"

"An ex-soldier, about your age, missing a foot, walks with a cane."

He'd forgotten how much he enjoyed the sound of her voice.

"You are not the most inconspicuous man that ever lived."

"I guess not. Who's looking?"

"A man in New York. A man you know."

"Giovanni."

She nods.

"What does he want?"

"What all mobsters *want*. You have cost him money. An entire neighborhood. He wants blood."

"Whose?"

She turns away, looks at the pond, the trees. "Do you remember taking me here, Patrick?"

"Of course."

She went to college at Middlebury. He accompanied her on the flight to New York. Drove her from the airport. Stopped to show him where he grew up. Vermont in September. Rosa, the desert flower was dazzled. By the colors of the leaves, by the smell of the trees, pine and maple. To her it was as exotic as Oz.

They stopped here. "Let me show you the most beautiful place in Vermont," he said.

He still thinks of it that way. A perfect place for exploring, for camping, for hunting, perfect place to bring a girl. To break up.

"It still makes me sad to come here," she says.

"Me too."

"I was so young."

"I know."

"Too young. You were right."

He wonders how much she's changed. What's left of the girl he knew. The girl he loved. "I wish I wasn't."

She lifts her eyebrows as though surprised he is still there. "My father never recovered, you know. He loved you too."

"He was a good man. In his way."

"In his way... You were always good with words, Patrick."

He remembers her offer. To run away. Empty their bank accounts and disappear. To Europe. Some exotic island. A child's fantasy. But what if he'd done it? How many people would be alive now?

"You remember my offer?"

Donovan closes his eyes. Doubts he has the strength to tell her, no, again.

"It still stands. Come with me. Right now. To Mexico."

"What about them?" He opens his eyes again.

"What about them? What do you owe them? Just walk away. We could be so happy, Patrick. You know it's true."

Does he? Could they? Would his recently discovered conscience leave him alone? Let him sleep? Or would guilt's icy fingers on his heart wake him, keep him company in the middle of the night?

"Why can't we be happy, Patrick? What is that worth?"

He can't think of anything to say. Slowly, he shakes his head. He can tell from her expression it is the answer she expects.

She steps close. He notices every beautiful detail of her face.

"Still my Don Quixote, my knight errant saving damsels in distress from dragons." Rosa summons the man in the woods.

Alejandro glides out of the trees. Nods his head at Donovan. "Amigo."

Rosa comes closer still. "Either way, you will never see them again. If you change your mind, you know how to find me." She kisses him lightly on the lips. Turns. Walks away.

He watches her as Alejandro begins to talk. Watches

her move between the trees, up the hill, get smaller, and smaller.

"I prefer to think of you as Johnny Silver."

"Okay."

"So, tomorrow."

"What?"

"We handle this tomorrow."

"Here?"

A chuckle. "No. There. Boston."

Donovan lets out a long sigh. "What if we're not there?"

A shrug. "What would you do?"

Hunt them down. Kill all of them instead of one.

"That's what we will do. I think you will be there. Or they will be. Your decision, amigo."

"You think I'm coward enough not to be there?"

"I know you're not a coward. Choosing one's own life over another's. This is not cowardice. This is living."

Alejandro holds out his hand.

Donovan shakes it.

"Until we meet again." He follows the same path as Rosa, into the forest, over the hill. He moves as quiet as death. Murder is often loud. Death is quiet.

TWENTY-TWO

—

THE LAST SUPPER, Donovan thinks to himself. Had he been on death row, able to request any meal, this would have been it. His mother's chicken cordon bleu, the chicken moist and perfect, wrapped around thinly sliced ham and Swiss cheese. He moans in approval, savors every bite.

His brother looks well, sleepy-eyed and content. Seems genuinely pleased to see Patrick. He tells stories about their childhood. About his brother, the wild stubborn boy he used to be. Their parents chuckle, adding occasional details.

Kate sips her wine and seems to relax. Donovan savors her expression as much as the food he tastes. Maybe more.

When he returned from the woods, Andrew's eyes were nervous. Donovan put a hand on his shoulder. "All settled. Don't worry."

Now the boy giggles milk out of his nose at the story of when Patrick cracked his head open sledding.

"There was so much blood, I couldn't tell where he was hurt."

For dessert, his mother's famous banana cream pie, crust and whipped cream from scratch. Patrick enjoys the looks on Kate's and Andrew's faces after the first bite, when it sinks in, that this is the best thing they've ever tasted. She made two pies. Everyone has seconds. Nice, strong coffee to wash it down.

When they are done, Kate helps Mrs. Donovan clear and clean the dishes.

Patrick and his brother take a walk around the yard in the long shadows of dusk. Don't say much. Don't need to. His brother smokes a Marlboro.

"Still doing that?"

He shrugs. "Only when I come here without the wife and kids. Makes it taste better actually, not doing it that often."

"How's the family?"

"Good, bro. You should try it. Looks good on you."

Patrick smiles, feels a tug in his chest but knows that ship has sailed. "So, look," he hands a piece of paper to him.

"What's this?"

"A couple bank accounts. I paid off mom and dad's house a few years ago."

His brother's eyes widen.

"I didn't tell them. You know Dad and his fucking pride."

"Yup."

"So their mortgage payments have been going into this account. Remember Kevin Joyner?"

"Sure."

"He's the bank manager here. He took care of it."

"Okay."

"I was just thinking. You should know about it."

"In case something happens to you?"

"In case whatever."

"Something going on with you?"

"Nope."

"Okay." He finishes his smoke, grinds it out on the heel of his boot.

It's nice to be with someone who knows you're lying and doesn't care why.

"How long you sticking around?"

"Just tonight."

"Too bad. Jenny and the kids would've liked to see you."

"That would've been nice."

"You still living in Vegas?"

"Now and then."

His brother smiled. "My brother. Man of mystery." He stuffed the paper with the account numbers on it into his coat pocket.

"You run into trouble, you're authorized to access that cash, bro."

"Thanks. At the moment we're doing okay."

"Good." He's never been so jealous of his brother. Would love to be his kind of 'okay.'

Andrew does not squawk about his bedtime. Patrick's parents retire shortly after. He and Kate sit in the living room, next to each other on a red and green plaid couch. This couch had witnessed more than a few make out sessions in high school.

"Your mom makes a mean pie."

"Yes, she does."

"What's wrong?"

He can't look at her. Looks at the wall, at a picture of him and his family, a relic from the seventies, their haircuts all wrong, the colors of their clothes all browns and oranges. If he stares at it long enough, could he return to that time?

"What is it?"

"We were there to kill the president of Afghanistan. Me and Crash and Doc and Nelson. That was the mission. Off the books."

"Please don't do this."

A picture of his parents, decades ago in some apple orchard, smiling. "I guess some Afghan soldier had a bead on me. Just trying to protect his president. A hero no matter where he's from."

"Oh God."

"Chris noticed. Killed the soldier. Saved my life."

"Why are you telling me this?"

"You need to know." He clears his throat. "I missed the president. Instead I hit a thirteen-year-old girl." Tears. How about that. "She didn't make it."

He can feel her shoulders drop, sense the small tremors of her weeping.

"Get away from me."

He nods, stands, walks to his old bedroom. Full of memories, this room, where he did most of his childhood dreaming. Donovan remembers his romantic notions of what soldiers were, what combat was like. In love and war, reality can never live up to the fantasy. In his experience, reality is always more painful. He lies in his old bed, feet dangling off the end. He waited out many sleepless nights in this bed. Always pining after something. A girl. The chance to escape.

Here he is again. Pining after a girl he can't have. Wishing he could escape his fate. Nothing new under the sun. The walls and shelves are decorated with plaques and trophies from his boyhood. Baseball and football. State championship banners. Team photos. A room filled with the ghosts of children.

What would that boy think of Donovan now? Would he thank him for fulfilling so many childish dreams? Or would he run screaming?

The girl visits him. Another ghost. She studies the pictures, the faded smiles of the boys. He tries to picture what she might look like when she smiles, but he cannot remove the pain from her face, any more than he can remove the pain from her heart.

She looks at him, her eyes sad.

He tries to wake himself up, then realizes, he isn't asleep.

A breakfast of buttermilk pancakes and maple syrup, Canadian bacon and home fries, strong coffee. Andrew is in his glory, his appetite ravenous. Mrs. Donovan observes this with a smile. Bob reads the Rutland Herald, mumbling to himself about politicians. Kate will not look at Donovan. He doesn't give her much reason to. It is what he wanted, but it still hurts.

"Are you sure you can't stay another day?" his mother asks.

"Just a quick getaway, mom. Thanks for having us."

Hugs all around.

"Kate and Andrew, this is when I normally tell guests to come back any time," his father says. "But with you two, I actually mean it."

As always, Donovan embraces both his parents like it will be the last time, concentrating on their scents. Is it his imagination or are they doing the same thing?

A quiet ride back to the motel where the other car is parked.

"Are you coming back with us, Patrick?"

He looks at Kate.

"Honey, Patrick's gotta get back home."

The boy gets choked up. Tries to hold it back so Donovan can't see.

"I'm gonna miss you, Andrew." Patrick has to strain to keep the emotion out of his voice.

He tries to take comfort in the fact that he is doing this for their own good. He has been given a cruel glimpse of a life that could have been. He knew it was possible, had seen his parents live a life of contentment – but he'd never wanted it, never understood it, until now. A life spent burning bridges had made it impossible.

"Okay, Andrew, get in the car."

They shake hands.

"You take care of your mom, kid."

Andrew walks outside, to the car.

When the door shuts after the boy, Kate moves close to Donovan, eyes awash.

"I'm sorry," he says.

She kisses him, quick, lips closed tight, a slight taste of salt. Donovan is too stunned to react. She looks at him again, her face a twist of sad and angry. The slap is hard and loud, catches him on the jaw.

"Goddamn you, Patrick Donovan."

She is gone before she can hear his reply.

"Soon enough."

TWENTY-THREE

—

GHOSTS IN THE CAR. He is never really alone. They keep him company all the way back to Boston. The girls is in the passenger seat, quiet, stares at the road ahead. Occasionally she turns to look at Donovan. When he looks in the rearview mirror, Chris Rogers' eyes are there, glaring.

"You got something to say, Chris?"

"What? You want some sympathy, Donovan? Gonna play the martyr? Spare me. I've already played that part. You ruin my life, then you ruin my family's life – turn my kid into a goddamned killer— you're a cancer, dude."

Donovan feels the small, cold fingers of the girl next to him as she takes his hand.

Chris is still talking. "Like a disease, you leave a trail of bodies in your wake. You try to do the right thing and you just make it worse. Just pave the road to hell.

You want to do me a favor, Donovan? Don't do me any fucking favors."

He thinks long and hard about returning to the desert, to Vegas, or Mexico. Pictures a life with Rosa, decadent and violent, thrilling but empty. He knows these ghosts would accompany him. All the way to hell. And new ghosts would join them. His conscience is getting too crowded.

These thoughts are never more than fantasies. Daydreams to pass the time. He knows where he is going and what will happen. What has to happen. The ghosts know it too.

He needs to get there before Kate and Andrew. Figures they'll take the easy way, stick to the major roads. Donovan takes every short cut he can think of, floors it the entire way. Stop signs and red lights are optional. Can't be late for this very important date.

As he nears the city, he doesn't get more anxious. The warrior in him takes over. He stops at a liquor store. A pint of Tullamore Dew. Spends fifteen minutes stretching, loosens his back, his shoulders. He checks his nine millimeter, holsters it. A few sips of booze while he rolls his neck, feels a popping in his neck.

Here we go.

He arrives just before five, the sky in full twilight, a breath of sun in a gray sea. The golden hour has turned copper. A few anxious stars already peek at the city. The car screeches to a halt in front of Kate's store. He wants people to notice. They do. They watch as he swaggers to the front door, unlocks it and strides inside.

He beat Kate and Andrew here, he takes a relieved breath. With luck, this can be wrapped up before they arrive.

He keeps the lights off, lets his eyes adjust to the dim emergency light. Alejandro's first wave should be here soon. Any second. He hears soft steps behind him and smiles. They are already here. With a swift lunge, Donovan turns the overhead lights on. The front window is suddenly a mirror. He sees the two wiseguys creep down two separate aisles. Then he turns the lights off, listens for movement.

The pistol in his hand explodes and the closest man goes down. The second man, sensibly, runs to the back of the store, but Donovan is expecting it and is at the end of another aisle first. A bullet to the head. A body on the floor.

He walks to the front door. Peeks his head out. "Next," he hollers.

Then ducks back, just avoids the bullets that shatter the glass. Donovan counts four muzzle flashes. He fires at the two on the left, thinks he hears the clatter of weapons hitting cement, hopes that's what it is. There'll be more in the back.

He turns, catches a shot in his left arm. A wicked sting. A flesh wound, but plenty of blood. He would run if he had two good legs.

He braces for the bullet, thinks, *Shit. Is this it?* A bullet comes, from the wrong direction. His attacker's face explodes, the now lifeless body tumbles to the ground.

Doc pretends to blow smoke away from the barrel of his pistol.

Donovan chuckles, "Doc, you dumb motherfucker. What are you doing?"

More gunshots. Nelson and Crash fire toward the front of the building.

"The cavalry done arrived, Captain," Doc says and goes stiff.

A bullet passes right through Doc's neck, in one side, out the other, blood spurts crimson. He spins in pain sending spirals of red fluid in a circle around him.

Nelson and Crash keep shooting.

"Fall back!" Alejandro's voice.

Donovan kneels next to his friend, cradles Doc's head in his lap. Warm blood stains everything, his clothes, his hands. Doc's eyes seem to swim in water, then find Donovan. He grins.

"Tell me what to do, Doc."

A bit of blood at the corner of his smile. Another of Donovan's men fading away.

"Fight the good fight, Captain. That's all we can ever do."

Doc's chest stills, his eyes stop quivering, turn into

rocks, all of him goes slack, his last breath a cold sigh from his lips.

Nelson and Crash next to him now. All he can think is, *not them. No more of his men. No more dying.*

From outside, Alejandro's voice.

"Johnny Silver? *Amigo*? Someone wants to say, hello. Go ahead, *hermanito.*"

"Patrick?" A choked whisper from Andrew.

"I'm listening," Donovan says.

"Walk outside. Hands up. Now."

Alejandro has Andrew in a loose, one-armed hug. Kate is nearby, quietly hysterical.

"Okay. Let him go. Do what you have to do."

"Your friends too."

They walk out, unarmed.

"On the ground, *por favor, señores.*"

Crash and Nelson know the drill. They lay on their stomachs.

Alejandro turns to Donovan. "We understand the deal, amigo?"

He nods.

Alejandro lets the boy go. "Take him away, *mamacita.*"

Kate pulls at Andrew but he won't go.

"This is where it ends. With me," Donovan says.

"*Sí, Señor.* Perhaps you would like to try your luck? An old fashioned gun duel?"

"What?"

"Like real cowboys."

"And if you win?"

"You die. We leave. The whole neighborhood."

"If I win?"

A devil's grin. "In that unlikely event, you still die. But we still leave. And I'm food for worms."

"What have I got to lose?"

"Precisely."

Donovan rolls his right shoulder.

Alejandro cracks the knuckles of his shooting hand.

"This is why you told me," Kate says.

Donovan doesn't answer. Doesn't look at her or Andrew.

Alejandro turns to her, bows his head. "He tried to make it easy on you. Make you hate him, maybe? Not miss him so much."

"Call it!" Donovan shouts.

Alejandro's attention returns to his opponent. Lean and mean, his eyes as blank as marbles, a perfect murderer.

He remembers seeing that look in the mirror. Killing eyes. The eyes of a hawk, arrogant, king of the skies. Donovan lost those eyes somewhere, started caring about the world again.

"*Uno.*"

A list of the things he will miss occurs to him.

"*Dos.*"

The people he has killed crowd the city street, jostle

for position, except the girl from Kandahar, front and center, she wears a look of resignation.

Donovan is dead before Alejandro finishes saying, "*Tres.*" Shot in the heart.

The ghosts crowd close. The young girl holds his hand, maybe she never stopped. A song on her lips, familiar to his ears. Had she been singing it all along? Like the white noise of crickets or a soft rain, something beautiful he'd grown numb to. Numbness in his fingers – touch and smell and taste are gone, pain too, and he misses even that. He is aware of his body in revolt, the fluids pumping out of his chest. It should hurt.

The world of living, breathing people slows. The moment of his death expands, freezes. He observes their faces.

The rush in Alejandro's eyes, the hunter's high that comes with a kill.

Crash and Nelson learning once more, the painful price of caring, the penalty for sticking your neck out.

The hardness in Kate's expression comes straight from her heart, she will not make the mistake of falling for anyone ever again.

Fascination and confusion wrestle across Andrew's face, an understanding learned too young.

The gunshot is a ceaseless echo.

Then he stands, looks down at the mess of his corpse. And he knows everything. Knows his parents will be sad but not surprised, knows Kate will pretend to forget him but never will, knows Alejandro will keep his word, the neighborhood will be left alone. Knows that good and bad are just words, like Heaven and Hell, like beauty, like truth – all in the eyes of the beholder.

In the end, he knows now, all we can do is behold.

ACKNOWLEDGMENTS

—

Nothing happens in my life without the support of my wife, Lisa. This book is no different.

Thanks to my publisher, Ron Earl Phillips, for picking this manuscript out of the pile.

Thanks to my first readers, Joe Clifford, Bracken MacLeod and Joe Gannon.

MIKE MINER lives and writes in New England. He is the author of *Hurt Hawks* (Shotgun Honey Books), *Prodigal Sons* (All Due Respect Books), *The Immortal Game* (Gutter Books) and *Everything She Knows* (SolsticeLit Books). His work can be found in the anthologies, *Protectors: Stories to Benefit PROTECT* and *Pulp Ink 2*, as well as *Beat To A Pulp, All Due Respect, Burnt Bridge, Narrative, PANK, Solstice*, and others.

ABOUT
SHOTGUN HONEY BOOKS

—

Thank you for reading **Hurt Hawks** by Mike Miner.

Shotgun Honey began as a crime genre flash fiction webzine in 2011 created as a venue for new and established writers to experiment in the confines of a mere 700 words. More than a decade later, Shotgun Honey still challenges writers with that storytelling task, but also provides opportunities to expand beyond through our book imprint and has since published anthologies, collections, novellas and novels by new and emerging authors.

We hope you have enjoyed this book. That you will share your experience, review and rate this title positively on your favorite book review sites and with your social media family and friends.

Visit ShotgunHoneyBooks.com

SHOTGUN HONEY
FICTION WITH A KICK